# A FOREVER FAMILY

# Sandi Lynn

*Sandi Lynn*

# A Forever Family

Copyright © 2015 Sandi Lynn

All rights reserved. No part of this publication may be reproduced, distributed, or transmitted in any form or by any means, including photocopying, recording, or other electronic or mechanical methods without the prior written permission of the publisher.

This is a work of fiction. Names, characters, places and incidents are the products of the author's imagination or are used factitiously. Any resemblance to actual events, locales, or persons, living or dead, is entirely coincidental.

Cover Design by Cassy Roop @Pink Ink Designs

Stock Photo: Image ID 147431333

Copyright: jfk image

www.shutterstock.com

Editing by B.Z. Hercules

*A Forever Family*

# Are You Ready?

## Table of Contents

Chapter 1...... 6
Chapter 2...... 12
Chapter 3...... 18
Chapter 4...... 26
Chapter 5...... 31
Chapter 6...... 38
Chapter 7...... 45
Chapter 8...... 49
Chapter 9...... 60
Chapter 10...... 70
Chapter 11...... 76
Chapter 12...... 83
Chapter 13...... 90
Chapter 14...... 97
Chapter 15...... 105
Chapter 16...... 113
Chapter 17...... 119
Chapter 18...... 125
Chapter 19...... 135
Chapter 20...... 141
Chapter 21...... 149
Chapter 22...... 156
Chapter 23...... 162
Chapter 24...... 168
Chapter 25...... 175
Chapter 26...... 182
Chapter 27...... 187
Chapter 28...... 192
Chapter 29...... 199
Chapter 30...... 204
Chapter 31...... 213
Chapter 32...... 219
Chapter 33...... 226

*A Forever Family*

Chapter 34 ................................................................................ 231
Chapter 35 ................................................................................ 236
Chapter 36 ................................................................................ 244
Chapter 37 ................................................................................ 249
Chapter 38 ................................................................................ 257
Chapter 39 ................................................................................ 262
Chapter 40 ................................................................................ 271
Chapter 41 ................................................................................ 275
Chapter 42 ................................................................................ 283
Chapter 43 ................................................................................ 291
Chapter 44 ................................................................................ 296
Chapter 45 ................................................................................ 298
Chapter 46 ................................................................................ 302
Chapter 47 ................................................................................ 306
Chapter 48 ................................................................................ 314
Chapter 49 ................................................................................ 318
A Special Thank You ............................................................... 320
About The Author .................................................................... 322

# Chapter 1
## Collin

Panic. Disappointment. Yelling. Crying. I could hear my mom's voice in my head, not to mention my dad's. Family was everything to them. Not to say that it wasn't to me because my life was my family, and now, my life was Amelia. They would have to understand. Would they understand? My dad, maybe because he knew. He got it. The connection. The love. The need to be with the one you were meant to be with. My mom, on the other hand, not so understanding.

*Shit.* I looked over at Amelia as she lay asleep. She looked so beautiful and she was my wife. My parents would have to understand. They'd get over it, eventually. This was my life, not theirs. Maybe I didn't have to tell them we were married. We could come back from Vegas and tell them we were engaged and they'd never have to know. Except we'd spend the rest of our lives celebrating two anniversaries. One in private and one with the family.

"Good morning." Amelia smiled as she ran her finger along my chest.

I kissed the top of her head. "Good morning, baby. Did you sleep well?"

"Of course I did. Someone wore me out last night."

I smiled as I flipped her on her back and hovered over her. "Is that so?" My lips brushed against hers in a passionate kiss. "I do believe that my wife took control and wore herself out."

She shrugged. "That's what my sexy husband does to me."

My phone rang and I sighed. I climbed off of Amelia and took it from the nightstand. It was my dad. My stomach twisted in knots.

"Hey, Dad."

"Good morning, son. What time will you be coming back today? Your mom wants the family together for dinner tonight."

*Shit. Shit. Shit.* I rubbed my forehead. "Tell Mom not tonight. The plane isn't even picking us up until noon and by time we get back to New York, with the time difference, it'll be close to eight o'clock. We'll be jetlagged and I have to be at the office in the morning and Amelia has an early class before her clinicals start."

"I understand, son, and I'll let your mom know." I heard him sigh. "She won't be happy, but she'll have to understand."

"Thanks, Dad. Ask her if we can do it tomorrow night."

"I will. Have a safe flight home and I'll see you at the office tomorrow."

I hung up and set the phone down on the nightstand. I climbed on top of Amelia and softly kissed her lips. "Now, where were we?" I smiled.

****

We walked into the apartment and set our bags down. It felt good to be home.

"Welcome home, Mrs. Black."

"Thank you, Mr. Black." She kissed me.

There was a knock at the door and Amelia and I looked at each other. I shrugged and opened it.

"Welcome home." Julia smiled as she walked in with Brayden.

"Ah, Julia. What are you doing here?" I asked as I looked at Amelia. She and I both hid our hands behind our backs.

Julia glared at me. Suspicion was running through her head, I could tell. "I just left Mom and Dad's and when I stepped off the elevator, I saw you two walk in. I thought I'd say hi. What's going on?"

"Nothing's going on. Why?"

"You're acting weird. What did you do?"

I snorted, something I did when I was nervous.

"You snorted! She pointed her finger at me. Talk to me, Collin. Amelia?" she said as she looked at her.

Amelia caved and held out her hand with her ring on it.

"OH MY GOD! You got engaged!" she exclaimed as she looked at her ring closely. She must have noticed the wedding band. "Wait a minute." She looked at me and grabbed my hand with my wedding band on it. Her eyes widened and she looked at me. "YOU GOT MARRIED?" she yelled rather loudly.

"Shh."

Brayden started to cry.

"Here, let me take him," Amelia said as Julia willingly handed him over to her.

"Oh my God, Collin. Why? I mean, I'm happy for you. But, oh my God, Mom! Dad!"

I walked away, shaking my head. "I know. I know. But this isn't anyone's business. I love Amelia and we were in Vegas and I wanted to marry her and she wanted to marry me."

"Isn't anyone's business? Are you kidding me?"

"Okay. I shouldn't have said that." I sighed. "I'm scared, Julia. Mom and Dad are going to flip out."

"Damn right they are. You took a wedding away from them. You know what a control freak Mom is. You're her sweet boy." Suddenly, an evil grin took over her face. "Maybe you won't be her sweet boy anymore."

"Ugh, Julia. Stop it. You're making things worse." I sat down on the couch and buried my face in my hands.

She sat down next to me and hooked her arm around me. "I'm sorry, Collin. You know I love you. I am so incredibly happy for you and Amelia. I really am. I'm just scared for you." She laughed.

"Thanks."

"Aw, come here." She pulled me into her. "When are you telling them?"

"I don't know."

"Well, when you do, I'll be there for you. When Mom explodes, I'll do my best to calm her down."

"Thanks, sis."

"I'd better get Brayden home and to bed." She got up from the couch and hugged Amelia. "Welcome to the family. I truly am happy for both of you."

"Thank you." Amelia smiled as she handed Brayden over.

"You better take off that ring before you come to work tomorrow."

"I will. Have a good night, sis. I love you."

"I love you too, Collin." She walked out the door and I looked up at Amelia. She sat down beside me and placed her hand on my thigh.

"Do you regret getting married?"

My heart ached when she asked me that. I took hold of her hand. "Of course not. I wanted nothing more than to make you my wife and no apology will be made. My parents will just have to accept it and move on."

"What if they won't?"

"They'll be happy we're married. They love you. They just won't be happy that we didn't include them." I sighed.

"Do I have to be there when you tell them?" She smiled.

"Yes. If I'm going down, you're going down with me. Now enough talk about my parents. They are last people I want to think about when I'm about to fuck you for the first time in our home as my wife."

She took her bottom lip in her mouth as her seductive eyes stared into mine. "Mhmm. I like that idea." Her lips softly touched mine.

## Chapter 2
## Ellery

Life couldn't be more perfect. I was married to the man of my dreams, I had two beautiful grown children, a perfect son in-law, and a beautiful grandson. The art gallery was thriving better than we had ever imagined and Black Enterprises was strong and solid. Connor had talked about retiring and letting Collin take over, but he wanted to wait a couple more years. He still felt Collin needed to grow up a little bit. I disagreed, and we had our discussions about it, but I stood by his decision to wait.

"Good morning, baby." Connor walked into the kitchen and gave me a warm kiss.

"Good morning. Tell Collin when you see him at the office that dinner is at six o'clock sharp."

"I will. Don't worry." He took his coffee over to the table as I set his breakfast in front of him.

"I was thinking last night about Collin and Amelia and how we could be planning a wedding for them in the near future."

"Let's not rush them into marriage, sweetheart. I think Collin needs a couple more years before he even considers getting married. They both need to get settled into their careers first."

"I agree, but isn't the thought exciting? Watching our baby boy walk down the aisle, marrying the love of his life like Julia did."

"Where is Julia, by the way? I thought she was bringing Brayden by this morning."

"I'm right here, Dad." She smiled as she walked over and gave him a kiss on the cheek and he took Brayden from her arms. "You know I'm only a few minutes late. It's hard with Jake being out of town."

"Sorry, princess. I was just missing this little guy."

I poured Julia a cup of coffee and handed it to her. "Why don't you and Brayden spend the night here until Jake gets back?" I was hoping she'd say yes.

"It's fine, Mom. I'm more than capable of being alone with my son. But thanks for the offer. Jake will home tomorrow night."

"Well, I have a full day planned with this little one." I walked over and took him from Connor's arms.

"Elle. I wasn't done playing with him."

"Sorry, babe, but he wants his grandma. Don't you?" I held him up in the air and he smiled.

It was hard to believe that he was already six months old. Spring was settling in New York and I was excited to take him to Central Park.

"I have an idea, Julia. How about you pack Brayden an overnight bag and let him stay the night with us tonight? That way, you can have a night to yourself."

"How about I take you up on that offer tomorrow night when Jake gets home so I can spend the night alone with my husband?"

I gave her a smile. "That's an even better idea."

Connor finished his breakfast and got up from his chair. "Are you ready to head into the office, princess?"

"Yes, Dad. I'm ready." She walked over and gave Brayden a kiss goodbye. "Be good for Grandma, Brayden, and Mommy will see you later."

He cooed and smiled at her. I took his little arm and waved goodbye as they stepped into the elevator.

****

## Connor

"Good morning, son," I got up from my desk chair and walked around to give him a light hug.

"Morning, Dad."

"How was the rest of your trip in Vegas?"

"It was good. We had a lot of fun."

I walked back to my desk and sat down, crossing my legs. Collin planted himself in the chair across from me. He seemed different.

"What's going on with you?"

"Nothing. Why do you ask?" He gave me a strange look.

"I can't put my finger on it, but you seem different."

"No, I'm not. I'm the same Collin I was a few days ago."

"Okay. Maybe it's just my imagination. Oh, your mom said dinner is at six sharp tonight. Don't be late."

He got up from the chair. "We will be on time. I promise."

I gave him a small smile as he left the office. As I was looking over some documents that my new secretary, Cara, typed up, I noticed a lot of errors. I pushed the button on my desk phone.

"Cara, could you please come in here?"

A few moments later, the door opened and she walked in. "Yes, Mr. Black?"

"Have a seat please." I pointed to the chair. "As I'm looking over these documents, I've noticed a lot of typing errors. Did you even go through them before handing them over to me?"

She looked at me with her brown eyes, and as she chomped on her gum, she sighed. "I thought I did. I'm sorry, Mr. Black. Hand them over to me and I'll go through them again." She held out her hand.

Handing the documents back to her, I frowned. "You have until five o'clock to get them back to me."

She walked out of the office and shut the door. I missed Valerie and Diana. I hadn't been able to find anyone competent enough to fill their shoes and it was starting to piss me off. Why I let Collin talk me into hiring Cara, I had no clue. She didn't even have that much secretarial experience. I looked at the calendar and thought next weekend would be a good weekend to go to the Hamptons and open up the house for the summer. This was the time of year I loved. Spending weekends at the beach house with the family were times that I always treasured. Although this year would be different with Collin having his own house right down the street. I pressed the button on my desk phone again.

"Cara, please call the florist and have a bouquet of roses sent to my wife at our home."

"Will do, Mr. Black."

I pulled out my phone and sent a text message to Ellery.

*"I'm having roses sent to the house so you can use them as a centerpiece for the dinner table tonight."*

*"Thank you, babe. I was going to stop with Brayden on my way home from the park to get some. I love you."*

*"I love you too. I'll see you later. Send me some pictures of our grandson."*

Before long, Ellery had blown up my phone with the cutest pictures of Brayden; some by himself and some with her. As I stared at him, he reminded me so much of Collin. I sat back in my chair and thought about what Denny used to say.

"Connor, that son of yours is the spitting image of you. Brace yourself because I have a feeling you're going to be in for one hell of a ride as he gets older."

I silently smiled because he was right. Collin was the spitting image of me, not only in looks, but in personality and defiance as well. He had grown into a man before my eyes and already endured such heartache but also extreme happiness, and I couldn't have been more proud of him for the way he handled things. I didn't have any worries as far as the company was concerned once I retired.

## Chapter 3
## Connor

I left the office early and headed home to my wife and grandson. He was the highlight of my life and I couldn't wait to sit down and play with him. I stepped off the elevator and set my briefcase down. Walking into the kitchen, I stopped dead in my tracks when I saw the flowers sitting in a vase on the counter.

"What are those?" I asked.

Ellery turned to me and smiled. "Those are the roses you sent me. Care to explain, Connor?"

Anger rose up inside me as I stared at the dozen black roses before me. "I can't believe that Cara would send black roses. What the fuck is the matter with her?"

Ellery started to laugh. "I guess they are different, aren't they?"

"It's not funny, Ellery." I took them from the vase and threw them in the garbage. "Where's Brayden?"

"He's taking a nap." She walked over to me and placed her arms around me. "Don't stress out over the flowers. It's not a big deal." She reached up and kissed my lips.

"It is. Who the fuck sends black roses? I'm firing her. I can't take it anymore. I had to give her back some documents today because they were riddled with errors."

"Again?"

"Yes. There's no way she graduated high school. The black roses were the last straw." I walked to the living room and over to the bar for a glass of scotch.

"I hear our grandson cooing through the baby monitor. Why don't you go upstairs and get him? He'll calm you down."

I sighed as I set down my drink and went up to see Brayden.

****

## Collin

When I came home, Amelia was in the bedroom changing out of her scrubs. I loosened my tie as I walked over and gave her a kiss.

"Hey, baby. How were clinicals?"

"They were good. How was your day?"

"Not bad." I stripped out of my suit and pulled a pair of khakis from the closet. I stared at my beautiful wife as she stood there, thumbing through her clothes in nothing but her bra and panties. I leaned over and brushed my lips against her soft neck.

"You smell so good. I'm getting hard."

She giggled as my tongue slid up to the edge of her ear. "Down, boy. We have exactly fifteen minutes to be upstairs at your parents' house."

"Well, there goes that hard-on." I sighed.

Amelia laughed as she turned around and placed her hand on my chest. "Are you scared?"

"Yes. To be honest, I am."

"What happened to all that talk last night about them having to get over it?" she said as she pulled on a pair of black pants.

"That was last night. Now it's today and this is happening in fifteen minutes."

"Ten minutes now. You better hurry up." She pulled a short sleeve white cotton shirt over her head.

I grabbed a shirt from the hanger. "Let's make it five. If we're early, my mom will be happy. Let's keep her happy at least for a few minutes."

"Okay. Sounds like a good plan."

We put on our shoes and took the elevator up to the penthouse. As the doors opened, my dad walked through the foyer holding Brayden.

"Well, look at you two. You're early." He smiled.

"Hey, Dad."

He walked over to Amelia and gave her a kiss on the cheek. "Good to see you, sweetheart."

"Is that my sweet boy?" My mom came from the kitchen. She hugged me and kissed my cheek and then turned and did the same to Amelia.

"How was Vegas? Did you two have fun?" she asked with excitement.

"Vegas was great. We had an amazing time."

The elevator doors opened and Julia stepped into the foyer. "Hi, Amelia." She smiled and gave her a light hug. "Hey, little brother. There's my baby boy. Mommy missed you today." Julia walked over and tried to take him from my dad. "Daddy, give me my baby."

"Princess, we're having a little bonding time. You get him all night. Let me hold him a while longer."

Julia frowned and I let out a chuckle.

"Everyone in the dining room. Dinner is ready," my mom chimed.

I grabbed Amelia's hand and we went into the dining room and took our seats. Julia kept smirking at me from across the table. I decided to wait until after dinner to tell my parents about our marriage. I didn't want all the food my mom spent all day making to go to waste. Once we finished eating, Julia, Amelia, and my mom cleaned up while my dad and I took Brayden into the living room.

"There's something I need to talk to you about, son. Scotch?" he asked.

"Sure, Dad. What's wrong?"

"I need you to fire Cara tomorrow."

I set Brayden down in his playpen as my dad handed me a drink.

"What? Why?"

"How do I put this nicely? She's an idiot. She makes nothing but errors. She's on her phone all day, scrolling through Facebook and Twitter, and she sent your mother black roses."

I couldn't help it. I busted out into laughter. "What?! Are you serious?"

"Yes. I asked her to call the florist and send a dozen roses to the house and she sent black roses."

"Did you specify a color?" I asked with a cocky attitude.

"Anyone with a brain knows not to send black roses and I don't find it funny."

"I do. But why do I have to fire her? She's your secretary."

"Because you're the one who conned me into hiring her. So now you can fire her and I want it done first thing in the morning. I don't want her touching another thing in that office."

*Shit.* I couldn't believe he was making me fire his secretary. He was in a mood because of her. Of all damn days. The women walked in the room and Julia took Brayden from his playpen.

"So tell me what you two did in Vegas besides gamble," my mom spoke as she sat down on the couch. "Did you see any shows, do any shopping?"

My heart was beating at a rapid pace and I started to sweat. I could feel the beads of wetness forming on my forehead. I swallowed hard and took Amelia's hand.

"Actually, we did do something really amazing." I tried to smile casually, but in reality, it was a nervous smile.

I looked over at Julia, who was holding Brayden extra tight. She gave me a small nod.

"Amelia and I got married!"

"Very funny, Collin." My mom smiled.

"That's not even funny, son." My dad pointed at me.

I looked down. "I'm serious. We got married."

"WHAT!" my mom screamed as she got up from the couch and Brayden started to cry.

"You better be kidding, Collin," my dad said with seriousness.

"I'm not kidding. I'm sorry I didn't tell you sooner."

My mom put her hand over her mouth as she looked at my dad. She stood there and stared at me with a look that I had never seen come from her before. It was a look of hurt, deceit, and betrayal.

"How the fuck could you do something like that without your family!" she yelled.

"Mom, calm down," Julia said.

"Did you know about this?" She turned to her and snapped.

Julia's eyes widened as she looked at me. I softly shook my head at her.

"No, Mom. I didn't know. I'm just as shocked but getting upset isn't going to change things."

"Collin, I have never been more disappointed in you as I am right now." My dad turned away from me. "I can't believe you would go and do something so stupid." He slammed his drink down on the bar.

As much as I loved my parents, there was no way in hell I was going to stand there and let them talk to me like that.

"Stupid? You think me marrying the woman that I love more than life is stupid?"

"That's not what I meant," my dad yelled.

"How could you do this to us?" A tear fell from my mother's eye.

"Do what to you, Mom? Take away your dreams of planning the perfect wedding for us? I didn't want to wait to marry Amelia. I love her and I wanted her to be my wife. I'm sorry, but you and Dad of all people should know that. You know how it feels to be so in love with someone that you can't bear to be without them even for a split second."

"We understand that, son, but you should have waited," my dad spoke.

"Why? Why should we have waited?"

"Because I'm your mother and I wanted to watch my son get married!" my mom screeched.

"I'm sorry, Mom. Dad. But this is my life and I did what felt right for us. Amelia is my wife and I am her husband and it's done. If you want to throw us a wedding reception, that's fine. But I will not apologize for marrying the woman I love most in this world. She's my life. I'm sorry we hurt you. That was never our intention. We're happy with or without your support. Now if you'll excuse me, I need to get out of here and get some fresh air."

I pulled Amelia behind me and when we approached the door, I stopped and turned to my parents. "If Mom wasn't sick when you proposed to her, you probably would have done the same thing. The only reason why you waited was because Mom wouldn't commit until she knew she was going to be okay." We walked out of the penthouse. I knew damn well this was the reaction we were going to get, but I was still angry and sad. They were disappointed in me, but I was also disappointed in them.

## Chapter 4
## Ellery

I stood there with tears streaming down my face and my heart ripped in half. Connor walked over and wrapped his arms around me. I let him console me for a few moments and then I broke our embrace, walked over to the bar, and poured a shot of Jack. I threw it back and the slow and steady burn grazed the back of my throat. Connor paced back and forth across the room. The air was thick with tension and silence.

"I hope the two of you are happy," Julia snapped as she got up and put Brayden down in his playpen. "Did you see the look on poor Amelia's face? Not to mention your son's?"

"How the hell could he have been so stupid?" Connor raised his voice.

I placed my hand on my head to try and control the tears that were once again steadily rising up in my eyes.

"Why is he stupid? What did he do that was so wrong? He married the one person in the world that he loves most." Julia walked over to Connor and pressed her finger into his chest. "I am so disappointed in you, Daddy. And you too, Mother." Her eyes glared over at me. "Collin and Amelia got married, big deal. It's not the end of the world. For the both of you to be so selfish makes me uncomfortable."

"Princess, we're in shock!"

"Julia, how would you feel if Brayden came home one day and told you he got married?" I walked over to where her and Connor were standing and placed my arm around his waist.

"If he married the girl of his dreams and couldn't live without her and she felt the same way, I'd be happy for them. I wouldn't have called them stupid. Listen, I understand how you both feel, but you need to stop and think about how Collin feels."

"He's young. He should have waited." I began to cry.

"Why? He isn't any younger than I was when I married Jake and you were all for that. You both love Amelia, so I don't understand why you're behaving like this."

"We're hurt that he chose to do something so sacred and special without his family there," I spoke as my heart ached something fierce.

"He was very selfish," Connor chimed in.

"Wow, Dad. I think the two of you are the ones being selfish right now."

"Julia, we're hurt. Why can't you understand that?" I spat.

"I do understand, Mom. But you know what? You can't control everything that happens in life. You of all people should know that. Collin is a man who made an adult decision. He's not your little boy anymore."

"He'll always be my little boy, just like you'll always be my little girl."

"Think long and hard about this before you do any more damage to the relationship with your son and daughter in-law. I have to get Brayden home. I'll talk to you tomorrow."

She took Brayden from the playpen and walked out the door. The tears that I'd held back came rushing forth and spilled all over Connor as he held me tight and I buried my head into his chest.

\*\*\*\*

# Connor

Once Ellery and I calmed ourselves down, we grabbed a bottle of wine and a couple of glasses and climbed into bed.

"We should call them," Ellery said as I filled her glass.

"Not tonight. Everyone is upset and we all need to calm down."

"How could he just up and get married like that, Connor?"

I looked into her sad blue eyes and placed my hand on her cheek. "He's my son, Ellery, and we both know that he inherited more from me than he did you. I would have married you right there on that beach in California the night I proposed to you. I didn't want to wait, and if you recall, I kept pressuring you about setting a date. But being the stubborn girl you were, you wouldn't hear of it until we got the results back from your final treatment. I know how Collin feels because I still feel that way about you today."

"And I still feel that way about you, my love." Her lips softly brushed up against mine. "But still, Connor. Our son got married without us."

"I knew something was off with him today. I even asked him about it this morning and he said he was fine. He was acting nervous and I found it odd. I never dreamed in a million years he would have gotten married."

"I bet he hates us now," Ellery pouted.

"He doesn't hate us, but he's probably really pissed off and hurt."

"So is Julia. Can you believe she talked to us that way?"

I chuckled. "I do because she's your daughter, Ellery."

I grimaced at the light smack against my chest. "Can you believe both our children are married? It seems like yesterday I was holding Julia in my arms."

I sighed. "I know, baby. Where did the years go?" I took the wine glass out of her hand and set it next to mine on the nightstand.

"What are you doing, Mr. Black?" Her eyes gave off a glimmer of light.

"I'm going to make sweet love to you before we go to sleep and then, when tomorrow comes, we'll talk with Collin and Amelia and apologize for what we said."

"But—"

I brought my fingers to her lips and softly pressed against them. "No buts. If things were different and you weren't sick, we would have done the same thing and you know it."

"I suppose you're right."

"Of course I am." I smiled as I kissed her soft lips.

"Don't push it, Connor."

I hovered over her and held her arms above her head. "Oh I'm going to push it, Elle, and it's going to be hard and deep. That I can promise."

## Chapter 5
## Collin

I took off my pants and sat down on the edge of the bed, cupping my face in my hands. Amelia emerged from the bathroom and sat down next to me, placing her hand on my back and rubbing it softly.

"Are you okay? I hate seeing you like this."

I turned my head so I was facing her as my elbows stayed planted on my knees. "I'm fine, I guess. I knew they were going to be pissed, but to call what we did 'stupid' was crossing the line."

"They're in shock, Collin. They need time to process it all. You know people say things they don't mean when they're angry. Your family is so tight knit that I understand where they're coming from."

"So you think the things they said were okay?" I asked as I got up from the bed.

"No. I don't think that at all. Give them time. I've gotten to know your mom and dad over the last several months and they'll forgive us. They're hurt right now and they feel betrayed."

I sighed as I stared down at her and took her hands in mine. "I know. But I don't regret marrying you in Vegas and I never will. I love you so much."

"And I love you." The corners of her mouth curved into a beautiful smile. A smile that would be forever etched into my heart and soul.

I looked down at her as I ran my finger across her lips. "I want you so bad. You still owe me from earlier when you ruined my hard-on."

She grabbed my shirt and pulled me on top of her. "What are you waiting for, Mr. Black? You can have me anytime you want and I promise I won't mention—"

My mouth crashed into hers before she had the chance to say it. I could feel her smile against my mouth and it excited me even more. Making love to her as my wife was even better. She was mine and I was hers and no one was going to take that away from us, especially my parents.

\*\*\*\*

The alarm went off as I rolled over and put my arm around Amelia, giving her head a soft kiss as she reached over and shut it off. An uneasy feeling erupted inside of me, knowing that I'd have to face my dad today. I was still upset and I had no intention of talking to him, at least not yet. Hell, I didn't even know if he had any intention of talking to me. I sighed as I gave Amelia a light squeeze.

"Do we have to get out of this bed?"

"Yep. We sure do." She turned over, gave me a kiss, and then climbed out of bed. "I'll start the coffee."

I smiled as I watched her walk away in the silk nightie I had bought her in Vegas.

Stepping into Black Enterprises, my stomach was twisted at the thought of seeing my dad. I was in no mood and the first thing I had to do was fire Cara. When I walked up to her desk, she was sitting there on her phone. I shook my head.

"Is he here yet?" I asked in a stern voice.

"Nope."

"I need to see you in my office." I motioned for her to go in.

I followed behind and set my briefcase down on the chair next to my desk. I sat down and looked at her as she looked at her phone.

"Do you think you can put your phone away for two seconds and look up at me while we have a discussion?"

"Sure. What's up?"

"Things aren't working out and we need to let you go." I got straight to the point.

"What's the problem? I think I'm doing a great job." She chomped on her gum.

"You make consistent errors, you're on your phone all day, you chomp your gum like some wild animal, and you sent my mother black roses."

"Oh." She smiled. "Did she love them?" She was clueless.

I sighed because I didn't have time for her stupidity. "No, Cara, she didn't. Who sends black roses?"

"I thought it was cute, considering your last name is Black and all."

"Well, my father had a different opinion. And really? Did you just really say that?" I couldn't believe the mentality of this girl. I am never going to live this one down with my dad.

"Yeah. You didn't think it was cute?"

I rolled my eyes. "Cara, you're fired. Please go collect your things and leave or I'll have security escort you out."

"Whatever. I didn't like working here anyway. You're all really uptight and boring." She got up from her seat and I followed her out, making sure she didn't steal anything.

She collected her things and just as she was walking down the hallway, my dad was walking to his office. It was a shit morning already and I didn't need it to get any worse. I turned away, went into my office, and shut the door. Before I made it to my desk to sit down, the door opened.

"I take it you fired Cara?"

"Yeah." My nerves got the best of me as I prepared for his next words and took a seat at my desk.

"I think we need to talk, son."

"Sorry, Dad, but I have a meeting to go to in a few minutes." I picked up the files from my desk and got up from my chair.

He stood in the doorway with his hand on the knob and stared at me. "Fine. We'll talk later. I'm sorry, Collin." His voice was sincere.

"Yeah, well, I don't want to discuss it now." I walked past him and down the hall, heading to Julia's office.

*A Forever Family*

\*\*\*\*

## Julia

As I was sitting at my desk sipping on a cup of coffee, Collin walked in and sat down in the chair across from me.

"Good morning. How are you?" I asked with sympathy.

"I'm fine."

"And Amelia?"

"She's fine too, but I can tell she's just as hurt by Mom and Dad's reaction last night."

The sadness in his eyes was overwhelming and I hated seeing my brother like this. "Just to let you know that after you left last night, I told Mom and Dad off."

"You did?"

"Yep. I sure did, but you knew they were going to react like that."

He shifted in his chair. "I know, but I had a tiny piece of hope that they would welcome our marriage with open arms without calling me stupid."

"They didn't mean it, Collin. They're upset. Hopefully, they calmed down and had a chance to think about it last night."

"After I fired Cara, Dad came to my office and said we needed to talk."

"What did he say?"

"I didn't give him the chance. I told him I had a meeting to go to and I left the office."

I got up from my desk and walked over to him, giving him a kiss on the cheek. "You're going to have to face him at some point. Your office is right next to his." I smiled. "I have to get these designs down to the print department. Wanna come?"

He gave me a small smile. "No. I better get back to my office. Thanks, Julia, for sticking up for me and Amelia."

After dropping off the designs to the print department, I stopped by my dad's office. When I opened the door, I saw him sitting, facing out the window. He turned around.

"Good morning, princess. Are you here to yell at me some more?"

"No, Daddy." I walked over and kissed his cheek. "I wanted to know how you and Mom are doing."

He threw the pen down on his desk and shook his head. "We had a long talk last night. Your mom is still really upset, but she'll be okay."

"And you?" I asked as I poured myself a cup of coffee and took a seat.

"I understand to some extent and I don't blame him. I just wish he would have waited."

"We can wish till the cows come home, but it won't change anything."

"Till the cows come home, Julia?" He chuckled.

I shrugged.

"We'll make this right, princess. Don't worry. Are you still bringing Brayden over for the night?"

"Yes, Daddy. You and Mom can have your grandson all to yourselves tonight." I got up from my chair. "By the way, Collin told me he fired Cara. What are you going to do for a secretary? Are you calling the temp agency?"

He sighed. "No. I'm stealing Collin's secretary for the time being."

"Maybe Mom can come fill in for a while."

"That's not a good idea. I wouldn't get any work done if she was here. She'd spend more time in my office and on my desk than at her desk." He winked.

"Ugh. Why do you say those things? If you need me, I'll be in my office wiping what you just said from my mind."

"Bye, princess. Have a good day." He laughed.

I secretly smiled because I loved the way my parents still felt about each other after all these years and I hoped that Jake and I would be the same way.

## Chapter 6
## Connor

As I sat at my desk, I couldn't take the silence between me and my son anymore. I walked to the closet, grabbed my gym bag, and went to Collin's office.

"Grab your gym bag and let's go. We're hitting the gym."

He looked up at me and then looked back at his computer. "I can't. I'm busy."

"Bullshit. You're busy if I say you're busy. Work can wait. I can't, and we need to talk. Now get your bag and let's go. Ralph is waiting for us."

He sighed as he got up from his desk and grabbed his bag. The ride to the gym was silent. After changing into our workout clothes, we hit the treadmill.

"I'm sorry, son, and I want you to know that I fully understand why you married Amelia in Vegas."

"Somehow, I don't believe you, Dad. You and Mom said some really hurtful things."

"I know and we're sorry. We just need you to understand how hurt we are. Do you understand that?"

"Yeah, I do. But you need to understand how much I love Amelia and I didn't want to wait. I don't see what the big deal is. You and Mom can throw us a wedding reception if you want and we can celebrate."

"That's not the point. We weren't there to watch you and Amelia say your vows. We didn't get to witness one of the most important things you'll ever do in your life. We've been there for you, helped and watched you grow into a man and it's something we planned on and couldn't wait for. We couldn't wait to watch our only son marry the woman of his dreams. To witness the union of you two becoming one. I guess your mom and I are being very selfish people right now."

"You are, but so am I. I'm sorry, Dad, that I hurt you both, but I'm not sorry I married Amelia the way I did. I will never apologize for that."

"I know and I wouldn't either. You were right; I would have married your mom right on the spot when I proposed to her without giving my family a second thought. You're a lot like your old man whether you want to be or not." I gave him a small smile.

He smiled back. "I know I am and, to be honest, that's not a bad thing. I look up to you, Dad. I always have. How was Mom this morning?"

"She's still upset. I wiped a couple of tears from her eyes before I left for the office, but she'll be okay."

"Umm, Dad." Collin looked straight ahead.

"Oh shit. How did she know we were here?"

"Dad, she's got that look on her face. I'm scared," Collin expressed.

"So am I, son. Just keep running."

Ellery headed straight for us with a mad-as-hell look on her face. "So. I see you're having a talk with our son without me, Connor." She stood there with her hand on her hip.

I swallowed hard. "Ellery. How did you know we were here?"

"Collin's secretary, Laurinda, told me. I went to the office to talk to both of you, hoping we could get this resolved, and I find out you're having a gym session with him?"

Collin and I got off the treadmill and wiped our faces with towels. "Let's go into the locker room, Ellery. People are staring."

"I don't care if they're staring. This is my gym and if I want to yell in it, I will."

Collin walked over to her and hooked his arm around her, kissing her cheek. "Hey, Mom. Let's go and talk."

I let out a sigh of relief as she placed her arm around his waist and we headed to the locker room.

****

# Ellery

I stood there and stared at my son as sweat dripped down his face. He was my boy and nothing he could ever do would change how much I loved him. Even though I was hurt by his decision to get married without his family, I needed to accept the fact that he was happy and that was all that mattered. Seeing him after his break up with Hailey was, at times, too much to bear. When he found Amelia, I saw something in him that I never had before. It was the same something that I had when I met Connor. As much as I didn't want to admit it, I understood.

"Go clean yourself up and we'll talk after."

"Okay, Mom."

Connor walked over to me and wrapped his arms around me. "I'm so proud of you, baby."

"You're all sweaty, Connor." I broke our embrace.

"I thought you liked it when I'm all sweaty." He winked.

"I do. Just not gym sweat." I reached up and kissed his lips. "Go change."

He slapped me on the ass with his towel before walking away and I took a seat on the bench. A few moments later, both my handsome men walked towards me in their tailored business suits. As they stood there in front of me, I stared at them with a tear in my eye. Not only did they look so much alike, they acted alike and Amelia was the luckiest girl in the world to be loved by my son. Just as I was by Connor. I stood up and wrapped my arms around my son.

"I am truly happy for you, Collin, and I want you to know how much I love you. I'm sorry for yelling at you last night."

"It's okay, Mom, and I know how much you love me. I love you too and so does Amelia. We just want you to be happy for us."

"I am. I'm very happy for both of you. Please come to dinner with us tonight so I can apologize to Amelia and welcome her properly to the family. We can also discuss a date for the wedding reception your dad and I are giving you."

"Amelia and I would love to have dinner with you and Dad tonight. What time?"

"I figured you'd say yes, so I already made reservations at Per Se for seven o'clock." I smiled as I placed my hand on his cheek.

"Seven it is."

"Now that we have this settled, Collin and I need to get back to the office. What are your plans for the rest of the day?" Connor asked as we left the locker room.

"I'm going to stay here and get in a workout and then go over some things with Bobby. I'll see my two sweet men later." I gave Collin a kiss on the cheek and Connor a kiss on the lips and watched with contentment as they walked out of the gym.

I pulled out my phone and called Julia.

"Hi, Mom."

"Hi, sweetheart. Your dad and I are taking Collin and Amelia to dinner tonight. Would you and Jake like to join us?"

"So you've made up?"

"Yes. I came to my senses and had a talk with Collin. We'd love for you to join us tonight."

"That's okay. Jake isn't getting home until six o'clock and then he'll want to spend some time with Brayden before I ship him off to you and Dad tonight."

"Okay. Then we'll pick Brayden up after dinner. Thanks, Julia, for letting him spend the night with us tonight."

"You're welcome, Mom. I know tomorrow is Denny's birthday and it's going to be hard on Daddy. Using time alone with Jake was a good excuse. I think having Brayden there tomorrow with you and Dad, at least in the morning, will help him feel a little better."

"I think so too, sweetheart. I'll talk to you later. I love you."

"I love you too."

I sighed as I ended the call. Tomorrow was going to be a difficult day for us, but mostly for Connor. He was still mourning Denny's death and it had been emotionally difficult for him. I was hoping that he'd take the day off of work tomorrow and spend it with me and Brayden. He never read the letter that Denny wrote him. He said that he wasn't ready and some day he would be. I had a feeling that day would be tomorrow.

****

When Amelia and Collin walked through the doors at Per Se, I stood up and gave Amelia a big hug.

"I'm so sorry, Amelia, for my behavior last night."

"It's okay, Ellery. I totally understand. My parents would have been upset too."

I broke our embrace as I took her hands before sitting down. "I would love it if you'd call me 'Mom,' and I'm thrilled to have you as my daughter in-law. Collin couldn't have picked a better girl in the world to marry. Congratulations and officially welcome to our family, Mrs. Amelia Black."

"Thank you so much, Mom." She gave a tender smile.

"Excuse me, Elle; it's my turn." Connor smirked.

I stepped out of the way as he hugged her and welcomed her to the family.

"What about me?" Collin asked as he held out his arms.

"We already hugged you earlier." I winked.

He chuckled and we sat down and ordered a drink. We spent the next couple of hours talking about the wedding reception and how we were going to tell the rest of the family that Collin was already married.

## Chapter 7
### Connor

I awoke to the sound of Brayden crying. Ellery got up to get him and she brought him back to the bed and handed him to me.

"Say good morning to your grandpa." She smiled.

I took him from her and gave him a kiss. He was happy and full of smiles now that he was out of his crib.

"I'm going to get his bottle. I'll be right back." She leaned over and kissed my lips.

As I held him in my arms, I smiled as I thought of Denny. Today was his birthday and I missed him. I missed our talks, his smart-ass comments, but mostly, I missed his lectures. Ellery walked back in the room and handed me Brayden's bottle.

"Are you okay, baby?" she asked.

"Yeah. I'm okay. I miss him, Elle."

She reached over and put her arm around me as she stroked Brayden's head while I fed him his bottle.

"I know you do. I miss him too. But you know, he wouldn't want you to be sad. He already made that very clear after he died."

"I still can't believe he's gone. God, I would love to know what he would have thought about Collin getting married in Vegas." I gave Ellery a small smile.

"I know exactly what he would have said. 'Connor, that boy of yours is exactly like you. Get your head out of your ass and be happy for him. Embrace his marriage and happiness because you know damn well you can't blame him.'"

I laughed. "You're right. I can hear those exact words."

She gave me a squeeze as she laid her head on my shoulder. "I love you more and more every day, Connor Black."

I turned and kissed her forehead. "I love you too, baby."

Once Brayden was fed, Ellery took him downstairs so I could take a shower. We were going to spend the day together; just the three of us. Like it was when we just had Julia. After my shower, I wrapped the towel around me and walked over to the armoire and opened the top drawer where I had kept Denny's letter all these months. I slid my finger under the flap and took out the folded white paper. Sitting down on the edge of the bed, I slowly opened it.

*Dear Connor,*

*My son and my best friend. As you're reading this, I don't want you to feel any sadness. I'm in a good place and I've been called home to reunite with my beautiful wife, Dana. Your journey to becoming a man was something that I treasured my whole life. You know Dana and I could never have kids, but we felt like our life was full because you were like our son. I know things with your own father hadn't been easy for you, but as he gets older, you need to forgive him. People make mistakes and you of all people should know that. You've made your fair share throughout the years and you were forgiven more times than I could count. Life is all about family and accepting things we can't control. You need to see the beauty in all things that happen because even the biggest mistakes can turn out to be the best gifts in life. Acceptance, forgiveness, and love prevail over anything that life throws your way. I love you, Connor Black, more than words can say and I think I did a damn good job of guiding you and loving you through the years. You've made me extremely proud and I couldn't imagine a better man who deserved a wife and family as perfect as yours. Take care of Ellery, Julia, and Collin, and do right by them. So far, you've done an amazing job and I'll be watching over you from afar to make sure you continue to do so. Remember, my son, that I will always love you and one day we'll be reunited in the big sky. Now, toss this letter and be happy. Be happy for me that I'm back home and stop being selfish because you're sad. Give Ellery a big kiss from me and don't forget, I'm always around. If you need to talk about anything, just give me a shout. You'll feel better, I promise."*

*Love always,*

*Denny*

Ellery walked in the room and stopped when she saw the letter in my hands.

"Is that—"

"Yeah." I looked up at her.

She walked over to me, set Brayden in the middle of the bed, and wrapped her arms around me.

"I'm confused, Elle. Some of the things he says in this letter about my father don't make sense." I handed her the letter. "Denny knew that my relationship with my father was on the mend over the last few years, so I don't understand what he meant."

"I don't know, Connor. Don't read too much into it. It's Denny. He's probably just making sure you stay on the right track with your dad."

"I don't know. But something about what he said bothers me. Especially the part about acceptance. Almost as if he knew something I don't."

"Sweetheart, seriously, you're reading too much into his words. Come on and get dressed. Go spend some time with your grandson while I get ready and we can start the day off by going to breakfast." She kissed my cheek.

"You're right. Let me throw on some clothes." I took the letter from her and folded it back up. I slipped it back in the drawer and closed the armoire. Still, something about that letter seemed off to me.

## Chapter 8
## Collin

As I sat at my desk, my phone rang and it was Diana calling. I had called her yesterday to tell her about me and Amelia, but she didn't answer.

"Hello, Diana."

"Hi, Collin. I'm so sorry that I didn't get a chance to call you back yesterday. Joel and I were having dinner with some friends and by time I got home and with the time difference, it was too late."

"That's okay, Diana. I just wanted to tell you some news."

"What's going on?"

I took in a deep breath. "Amelia and I got married in Vegas last week."

There was silence on the other end. "I'm sorry, what did you say?"

"Sorry just to spring it on you like that."

"God, Collin. Congratulations. I'm so happy for both of you. Wait until I tell Jacob. He'll be thrilled. Your parents must have been so happy. But I am a bit surprised that you did it in Vegas."

"Well, we eloped. My parents weren't there and they didn't know until I came back to New York."

"Oh. How did they take the news?"

"Not good at all. There was some tension and hurt for a couple of days, but we talked and everything's cool now. My mom is planning a wedding reception and I want you and Jacob to come celebrate with us."

"We wouldn't miss it for the world. When is it?"

"We haven't set the date yet. But as soon as we do I'll let you know. How's Jacob doing?"

"He's doing really good, Collin. His attacks are few and far between now and he hasn't been hospitalized once since we moved here."

"That's great, Diana. I'm so happy for you both. Amelia and I are going to come and visit you guys next month. We talked about it last night."

"That's wonderful. We can't wait to see you."

"So." I paused for a moment. "How's it going with Joel?"

She laughed into the phone. "Joel and I are great. We are dating exclusively and I'm pretty sure I've fallen in love with him. The best part is the way he is with Jacob and Jacob loves him."

"Excellent." I leaned back in my chair. "That's what I like to hear." My office door opened and my dad walked in. I held up my finger. "Listen, Diana, my dad just walked into my office. I'll talk to you soon." *Click.*

My dad walked over to my desk.

*A Forever Family*

"Diana said hi. She and Jacob are doing really good."

"I know, son. I spoke with her last week."

I tilted my head and narrowed my eyes. "And you didn't tell me this, why?"

"Because someone decided to spring some shocking news on us and I didn't think about it."

I looked down. "Oh. Anyway, what are you doing here? I thought you were spending the day with Brayden and Mom."

"I am. I just had to grab a file from my office."

"Where are Mom and Brayden?"

"In Julia's office. We're taking Brayden to the Central Park Zoo."

No matter how hard my dad tried, he couldn't hide the sadness that overtook him today. I walked over to where he was standing and gave him a hug. "I miss him too, Dad."

"I know you do, son. We all do. He really left a mark on this whole family."

"He sure did."

"I better get going. I don't want to keep your mother waiting. I'll talk to you later."

I gave him a small smile as I walked him to the door. "Have fun at the zoo, Dad."

"Thanks, Collin."

After the workday ended, I grabbed my briefcase and headed home. When I walked through the door, an amazing aroma filled the air. I set my briefcase down and walked into the kitchen, where I found Amelia standing over the stove.

"Hey, baby." I wrapped my arms around her and slid my tongue across her neck.

"Mhmm. Hi." She turned around with a smile and wrapped her arms around my neck.

"What is that delicious smell?"

"I'm making a roast." Her lips brushed tenderly against mine.

"How much longer until it's ready?"

"About thirty minutes."

I stared into her eyes as the corners of my mouth curved into a smile. "Then we have time for sex."

"Not really. I have other things I need to prepare. I have to cut up the lettuce and vegetables for the salad. You can help me if you'd like."

"I would love to help. I'm going to change out of my suit and I'll be right back." I pressed my lips against hers.

I went to the bedroom and changed out of my suit and into a pair of sweatpants. When I walked back in the kitchen, Amelia was standing at the counter, cutting the lettuce. She looked so sexy in her cropped yoga pants and tank top. I couldn't resist myself. I wanted her and I was going to have her no matter what. I came up from behind and planted my hands firmly on her breasts.

"Collin. What are you doing?" She turned her head and gave me a small smile.

"Shh, baby. Just enjoy it." My lips softly caressed her neck as my hands made their way up her shirt, feeling her naked breasts.

I pressed my erection against her and a soft moan escaped her lips. As I took her hardened nipples between my fingers, she set down the knife and placed her hands firmly on the counter. She knew there was no stopping me. Her head tilted to the side so my mouth could have easier access to the soft skin of her neck. She reached back and placed her hand on my head.

"Keep both hands on the counter."

I released her breasts and hooked my finger in the sides of her yoga pants, taking them down with her panties all the way down to her ankles. I lifted each leg and removed her pants, tossing them to the side. My tongue slowly ran up the back of her leg. She gasped. As soon as my mouth reached her beautiful ass, I drew tiny circles around with my tongue as I dipped my fingers inside her. She was soaking wet already and my cock was twitching something fierce. Her breath hitched as I moved my fingers in and out of her, teasing her and bringing her to an orgasm the minute I pressed my thumb firmly against her clit from behind.

"Collin. Oh God. Collin," she screamed as I stood up and wrapped my arm around her waist, holding her tight as my fingers played with her while she climaxed. Once her orgasm subsided, she stood in front of the counter, panting. I pulled down my sweatpants, spread her legs, and thrust my cock in and out of her at a rapid pace.

Her moans became high pitched with each thrust. "Bend over a little bit, baby."

She did as I asked and I went deeper inside her, hitting all the right spots that made my cock twitch. With a firm grip on her hips, the warmth of her pussy, and three more pumps, I pushed deep and moaned as I released myself inside of her. Wrapping my arms around her, I buried my face into her neck as I tried to regain normal breaths.

"Okay, baby. I'm hungry now." I picked up the knife and started cutting the lettuce.

"What are you doing?" She laughed as I was still buried inside of her.

"Helping you with the salad."

"So we're cooking naked now?"

"You're not completely naked. You still have your shirt on. But I do like that idea."

"Collin," she whined.

"Okay. Okay." I pulled out of her and pulled up my pants.

"Can you please finish the salad while I go and clean myself up?" She turned around with a beautiful smile splayed across her face.

"I'll do anything for you, baby." I pressed my lips against hers before she headed to the bedroom.

****

The next day, I had a meeting across town. My dad was supposed to attend with me, but something came up at the office and he needed to stay behind. I was used to handling these meetings on my own. Sometimes, I wondered if my dad bailed on purpose just to sit back and watch how well I handled things

*A Forever Family*

without him. After the meeting was over, I had Ralph drop me off on Broadway, where I was meeting Julia at Artie's Deli for lunch. As I was walking down the street, two kids ran past me and bumped into a woman who was holding two brown paper grocery bags, knocking them out of her hands. Fruit and vegetables spilled all over the sidewalk. The little punks didn't even bother to stop and help her. I shook my head as I bent down and helped her pick them up.

"Damn kids. Are you okay, ma'am?"

"I'm fine. Thank—" She stopped mid-sentence as she looked up and stared at me. "Connor?" she narrowed her eyes.

This was weird. "No. My name is Collin. My father's name is Connor. Do you know him? Connor Black?"

There was something in her expression that seemed off. It was almost as if she was in shock or something.

"Oh. I'm sorry. I thought you were someone else. My apologies."

"Ah, okay." I smiled as I helped her pick up the rest of her food.

"Thank you, Collin, for your help. You're a very nice man."

"You're welcome. Have a nice day."

"You too." She walked away and continued down the street. I couldn't help but notice how nervous she seemed. It was strange, but I just shrugged my shoulders and made my way down to Artie's Deli.

When I walked in, Julia was already sitting down eating and my sandwich was on the table waiting for me.

"Hey, sis." I kissed her cheek.

"What took you so long? I went ahead and ordered your sandwich."

"A couple of kids knocked some groceries out of a woman's arms and her fruit and vegetables spilled everywhere, so I stopped and helped her pick them up."

"That was sweet of you."

"It was strange, though. When she looked at me, she called me Connor."

"Huh?" Julia narrowed her eyes.

"I asked her if she knew Dad, but she said she thought I was someone else. She seemed really nervous."

"That's weird."

"Yeah. I thought so too. Anyway, thanks for the sandwich."

"You're welcome." She smiled.

"I'm thinking about hiring my own driver. Thoughts?"

She arched her eyebrow as she sipped her water. "Why?"

"Because I don't want Amelia taking the subway. I can't always be there to pick her up and the cab drivers are crazy here. She was telling me last night how the cab almost got into an accident."

"What's wrong with Ralph?"

"He's Dad's driver and he's not available all the time."

"Then hire someone. I think it's a good idea. While you're interviewing drivers, you might as well interview secretaries for you too."

"I have a secretary." I took a bite of my sandwich.

"Oops. Dad didn't tell you yet?"

"Tell me what?"

"He's stealing Laurinda from you and you have to find a new secretary."

"My ass he is! Laurinda is a damn good secretary and he just can't take her from me."

"Yes he can. It's his company." She laughed.

I rolled my eyes and let out a sigh. This was shit and I'd be telling him how shit it was just as soon as I got back to the office.

\*\*\*\*

When I got back to Black Enterprises, my dad wasn't in his office.

"Laurinda, do you know where my dad is?"

"He's in a meeting."

I looked at her and flashed her my genuine sexy smile as I perched myself on the corner of her desk.

"You like working for me, right?"

"Of course, Collin."

"We've been through a lot, you and me, right?"

She narrowed her eyes at me. "You mean all the times I had to cover for you with your dad?"

I sighed. "Yeah. Something like that." I leaned in closer to her. "You'd never leave me, would you?"

"Does this have anything to do with me becoming your father's secretary?"

"So he's talked to you already?"

She laughed. "Yes and he's your dad. He owns the company, Collin. I have no choice."

"But you do have a choice, Laurinda. You can tell him no."

"He'd fire me."

"No he wouldn't. He'd make me fire you and I would never."

She laughed again. "Thank you for that, but I'll still help you out until you find my replacement."

I looked up and saw my dad walking down the hall. "Secretary stealer. We need to talk, Dad."

"Yes, we do, son. In my office, please." He chuckled.

I got up from Laurinda's desk and followed my dad into his office, taking the seat across from his desk.

"You can't have my secretary. It's not fair, Dad. You made me fire yours and now you're stealing mine? What happened to loyalty?"

"Collin. This is business and you'll find a new secretary. Plus, I'll be retiring in a couple of years and when you take over, you can have Laurinda back."

"I'm telling Mom."

"Your mom already knows. In fact, she suggested it."

"Wow. This is payback for getting married in Vegas. Isn't it?"

He sighed as he sat down in his chair. "Son, it's not payback. Now, I have some work to do. Call human resources and tell them to start looking for candidates. Once word gets out that Collin Black needs a new secretary, women will be lining up outside the building for the job." He smiled.

"This is the thanks I get for finding you Diana."

"You mean the one you made move to California?"

I sighed. "Okay. Okay. I'll go call human resources, but don't think I'm okay with this because I'm not." I walked out of his office and I heard him snicker.

## Chapter 9
## Ellery

"I'm throwing myself a birthday party," Peyton said as I handed her a glass of wine.

"Oh. And where are you having it?"

"Tenjune. We're going to have so much fun! Just like the good old days, Elle. It's Saturday night so you better not have plans."

"I don't have plans, but why the last minute?"

"I was waiting to see if Henry would throw me a party and he isn't. I came right out and asked him and he said he didn't think I'd want one. What the hell is wrong with him? He knows how much I love to celebrate my birthday."

Connor walked into the living room and gave me a kiss on the cheek. "What's this about a party?"

"Peyton is throwing herself a birthday party Saturday night at Tenjune."

"Ah. Nice. That sounds like fun." He smiled at her.

"You bet it will be. We're going to party all night long." She winked.

*A Forever Family*

Little did she know that Henry had already planned a surprise party for her at Pacha on Saturday night. After a couple more glasses of wine and a lot of laughing, Peyton left and I went upstairs to get ready for bed. Connor looked up from his laptop when I entered the room.

"Our son is very displeased with both of us at the moment."

"Why?" I asked as I took off my earrings.

"Because of Laurinda."

"Ah. I see. Well, he'll get over it. I can come and help him out until he gets a new secretary." I smiled.

"I don't think he wants his mommy sitting outside his office."

I turned around and gave Connor a stern look. "What's that supposed to mean? What's wrong with his mommy wanting to help out?"

He sighed. "Let me rephrase that for you, my love. I don't want you sitting outside his office. His office is next to mine, which means you'd be sitting outside my office as well, and to be honest, it would be too much of a distraction."

I smiled as I lifted my shirt over my head and took down my pants. I slowly crawled onto the bed and closed his laptop, taking it from his lap and setting it to the side.

"You mean this would be too much of a distraction?" I softly kissed his lips.

"Mhmm. Yes. Too much. I'd never get any work done." His hand moved over the fabric of my bra.

"It could be exciting." I straddled him and ran my fingers through his hair. "I could pretend I was your secretary and I could sit on your desk and take notes."

"I could fuck you on my desk as you took notes." His fingers unhooked my bra and his mouth traveled to my breasts.

"It wouldn't be the first time, Mr. Black."

"I'll think about it, Mrs. Black. Now lift up that sweet ass so I can take off those sexy panties."

\*\*\*\*

I stood and stared at myself in the full length mirror at the Valentino black sleeveless dress with the deep curving neckline and ran my hands down my side. Connor walked out of the bathroom with a towel wrapped around his waist and stared at me.

"Is that what you're wearing?"

I glared at him. "Yes. Why?"

"It's nice." He gulped.

"Nice? Is that all you have to say?"

"Yes, baby. It looks beautiful on you. Don't you think you'll be a little cold?" he asked as he walked into the closet.

"Why would I be cold? It's warm out."

"With the way your back is so exposed. I mean, there's not much to the back of that dress."

I rolled my eyes. "I'll be fine, Connor."

"What about the front? I mean, it's so low cut that your boobs might catch a draft," he said as he slipped on his shirt. "Plus, you're not wearing a bra and your nipples are hard. So you are cold. Maybe you should change."

"What exactly are you trying to say, Connor?" He knew better than to start an argument about the dress. Or at least I hoped he did.

He walked over and kissed my cheek. "You look stunning and I love the dress. I just wish there was a little more material, that's all. But if you love it, than so do I." He smiled.

"Good choice of words, baby. And my nipples are hard because I'm excited that you're staring at me and I know the dress is pissing you off, which is turning me on. Now hurry up and get ready. Is anyone driving with us?"

"No. The kids said they'd meet us at the club. And I'm not pissed off about the dress, Elle," I heard him say as I walked out of the room.

We walked into Pacha and it was crazy. Connor took my hand and led us up to the third floor where we saw the kids and a room full of other friends.

"Hey, Mom." Collin smiled as he kissed my cheek.

"Look at you, Amelia. You look gorgeous." I gave her a hug. We were wearing the same dress, but hers was red.

I saw Connor shoot Collin a look and he shrugged. "Good boy, son. Good boy." I smiled.

"No use, Dad. I've learned from Mom over the years and I'll never win. So I don't even bother saying anything."

Connor rolled his eyes and hooked his arm around Collin and led him to the bar for a drink. Henry had texted me earlier and said that he and Peyton would be arriving at seven thirty. I looked at the time on my phone and it was seven fifteen.

"Hey, Mom. You look amazing. Is that Valentino?" Julia asked as she hugged me.

"Yes. You look beautiful, darling."

I said hello to Jake and Connor handed me a glass of wine. The music was loud and I couldn't wait to start partying. Connor and I walked around and talked to some friends of ours, and when I looked over, I saw Hailey approaching us.

"Connor, Ellery, it's good to see you." She hugged us both.

"Hailey. It's good to see you too, sweetie. Your mom didn't tell me you were back from Paris."

"She doesn't know. I'm here for her birthday. It's a surprise."

"She'll be so happy. You look great. How have you been?"

"I've been okay." Suddenly, a handsome young man walked up to her and took hold of her hand. "Marcus, this is Connor and Ellery Black. This is Marcus, my boyfriend."

There was something about the way she said she was okay that didn't sit right with me. As much as she tried to seem happy, her eyes told a different story.

As loud as the club was, Peyton could be heard throughout the state of New York. I looked up and smiled when I heard her scream and begin jumping up and down, hugging Henry in shock that he threw her a party. I walked over to her and gave her a big hug.

"Happy birthday, my best friend in the whole world."

"Did you know about this? Did you, Elle? Because you didn't tell me, and I thought we had a code!"

I laughed. "I knew, but I wanted it to be a surprise. For once in your life, Peyton, I wanted you to be surprised."

****

## Collin

I stood at the bar and talked to Jake while Amelia and Julia went to the bathroom. My stomach twisted when I saw Hailey talking to my mom and dad. I hadn't talked to her since that day in the flower shop, except for a brief text message wishing me and Amelia a Merry Christmas. Our eyes caught and she gave me a small nod. *Shit*. I didn't want Amelia to be upset that she was here. When Amelia and Julia came back from the bathroom, she wrapped her arm around my waist and whispered in my ear.

"I saw her walk in and it's fine. Let's not make this awkward."

I kissed the top of her head and then took a sip of my scotch. I took it that Peyton didn't know she was going to be here because the minute she saw Hailey, she started to cry. We walked over to say happy birthday to her and to say hi to Henry.

"Happy birthday, Peyton." I smiled as I gave her a hug and kiss.

"Thank you, Collin. Thank you all for coming tonight."

Hailey placed her hand on my arm. "Hey, Collin. Long time no see."

"Hey, Hailey."

She looked at Amelia and gave her a smile. "I heard you two got married. Way to go. Congratulations."

"Thanks." I knew Amelia didn't want things to be awkward, but they were. It didn't matter how hard we tried, the history that Hailey and I once had would always make things awkward.

"This is my boyfriend, Marcus."

He extended his hand and I shook it. "Nice to meet you, man. If you'll excuse us, we're going to get another drink," I spoke as I led Amelia to the bar with me.

As the night went on, me, my dad, Jake and Henry were sitting around on the couch, drinking, talking, and watching our women on the dance floor.

"Dad, I think Mom's drunk."

"I believe she is, son. And I also think Amelia is."

"Yeah. That last mojito put her over the edge. I told her not to drink it."

I kept my eye on a guy who was hanging around on the dance floor and getting awful close to Amelia and my mom. Julia left to go to the bathroom and when she came back, she grabbed my arm.

"I need to talk to you now." She pulled me from the couch and into the corner by the bar.

"What?"

"I was just in the bathroom and I saw Hailey doing coke."

"Drinking a coke?" I asked as I leaned in closer to her.

"No, Collin. She was snorting cocaine."

"Seriously?" I narrowed my eyes.

"Yeah. I'm worried about her."

"Then talk to her, Julia. Don't involve me. I don't care what she does with her life." I walked away and sat back down on the couch.

My dad tapped me on the shoulder and then leaned into me. "See that asshole on the dance floor next to your mother and your wife?"

"Yeah. I've been watching him."

"I know exactly what he's going to do and the minute he does, we're taking him down."

Sure enough, a few moments after my dad said that, the guy stood behind my mom and Amelia and placed his hands on their asses. A flame erupted inside of me and I could tell by the look on my dad's face he was going to kill him. We both got up, grabbed the guy by the arms, and my dad pushed him up against the wall.

"I will rip your fucking throat out if you ever lay your hands on my wife and daughter-in-law again. Do you understand me?" He grabbed him by his shirt and shook him.

"Yeah. I get it, man. Back off."

My dad let go of him and, as we started to walk away, the guy spoke.

"They were asking for it. They look like whores. I bet if you weren't here, they'd be spreading their legs wide for me."

Without even thinking, I turned around and threw a punch, my fist smashing into his jaw. He fell against the wall. Grabbing his shirt and pulling him up, my dad's fist hit the other side of his face, knocking him completely on his ass. Security took the guy and escorted him out of the club.

"Still got it, Connor." Peyton smiled.

"Sorry, Peyton."

"Oh, please. I always did love watching you in action. Gotta love the Black men." She winked.

My dad hooked his arm around me. "How's your hand, son?"

"It's fine, Dad. How's yours?"

"It's fine."

"Connor, what the hell is the matter with you?" my mom slurred.

"Collin, what were you thinking?" Amelia asked with a stern look.

Did they not feel that man's hands on their asses? "Babe, he touched you inappropriately and I wasn't about to let him get away with it. What would you have done if some chick walked up to me and grabbed my crotch?"

Her eyes narrowed and she twisted her face. "I would have hit her."

"Exactly. So come on. Let's enjoy the rest of the night." I put my arm around her and pulled her into me. "Nobody touches your ass but me."

## Chapter 10
## Connor

The week had come and gone and we finally made it to the Hamptons. Julia and Jake joined us at the house while Collin and Amelia went to theirs. I was used to having the whole family stay at the beach house and knowing that Collin wouldn't be here bothered me. Ellery told me not to worry because they were right down the street and we could see them at any time. We got the house cleaned up, opened all the windows to air it out, and we were hosting our first barbeque of the season with our family and some friends.

I looked out the window and smiled when I saw Collin on his surfboard in the water and Julia and Jake sitting in the sand with Brayden. It seemed like yesterday that Collin and Julia were babies. I walked down to the water and watched Collin as he surfed. A few moments later, he got out of the water and set his board in the sand.

"What's up, Dad? Why are you just standing there?"

"Just taking in the ocean air and watching you surf. I guess I'm getting a little sentimental, that's all. You and your sister grew up way too fast. We had some amazing times here when you were little."

"We still do, Dad. Hey, I forgot to tell you. A couple of weeks ago, some kids knocked over a woman's groceries on the street, so I stopped to help her pick them up. She looked at me and called me Connor. I told her my name was Collin and that you were my dad. I asked if she knew you and she seemed really nervous. She said she had me confused with someone else."

"That's odd. What did she look like?"

"Around your age. Maybe a couple years younger. She had dark hair and green eyes. She was pretty attractive for an older lady."

My stomach twisted in the tightest knot possible and I swallowed hard. "Did you get her name?"

"No. Why would I?"

"No reason." I put my hands in my pockets as I stared at the water.

"I'm going to go get changed before Mom and Amelia get back from the grocery store. I'll see you soon."

"See you soon, son." I gave a nod.

I took in a deep breath as I pulled my phone from my pocket and dialed Frank.

"Hey, Connor, what's up?"

"I need you to find out if Ashlyn is back in New York."

"Last I heard, she was living in Texas after she got released from jail. Have you seen her or something?"

"No, but I think my son did. Get back to me as soon as possible."

"I'll get right on it, Connor."

I placed my phone back in my pocket as the burn in my blood became heightened. The last thing I needed was that bitch back in New York. It was bullshit that she was released from jail. She got out three years early because of good behavior and she sought therapy. I had been keeping tabs on her when she was first released to make sure she stayed out of New York. How the hell was I going to tell Ellery? I walked back up to the house and Ellery and Amelia had just pulled up. Jake and I helped bring in the bags while Julia put Brayden down for a nap and went over to Collin's.

\*\*\*\*

## Julia

I walked into Collin's house and he had just gotten out of the shower. I yelled up the stairs that I was here and that I needed to talk to him. After he finished dressing, he told me to come up to the bedroom.

"What's up, sis?"

"I met Hailey for dinner last night."

"So?"

"She was as high as a kite."

"I already told you that I don't care. What she does with her life is her business. It's not mine."

I sat down on the bed and sighed. "You two were best friends and dated for six years. You're not going to tell me that you don't even care just a little bit."

*A Forever Family*

He looked at me with the same look my father gave me when he was trying to figure out what to say. I silently smiled.

"Listen, Julia. If she wants to go down that road and ruin her life, there's nothing I can do. What makes you think she'd listen to me anyway? In fact, what the hell do you want me to do?"

"Talk to her. I don't like that guy she's with either. There's something about him that bothers me."

"Tell you what. I'll just have my ex-girlfriend, who up and left after six years and cheated on me, and my wife sitting at the dinner table together and we'll all pretend we're best friends."

"I didn't say you had to involve Amelia."

"Involve me in what?" Amelia asked as she walked into the room.

*Shit.*

"What's going on, Collin?" she asked as she shot him a look.

He sighed. "Apparently, Julia saw Hailey doing a line of coke in the bathroom at Peyton's birthday party and she had dinner with her last night and said she was high. She wants me to talk to her."

"I don't think talking to her is going to help. If she has a drug problem, she needs to be the one to want to stop. It doesn't matter how many people try to intervene."

"See?" Collin said with a raised brow.

I got up from the bed. "Okay. Just forget I mentioned it." I walked out of the room.

"Julia, wait," Collin spoke as he came after me. "I know why you're so concerned and I'm sorry. Don't forget, I was with you when you found out about London and I was there for you every step of the way."

"It's fine. I just don't want to lose another friend." I walked out the door and headed back to the beach house where I helped my mom and dad prepare for the barbeque.

The minute I walked into the kitchen, silence overtook the atmosphere. I could tell my parents were in a heavy discussion and they didn't want me to know about it.

"What's going on? Why did you stop talking when I came in?"

"It's nothing, princess." My dad gave way to a fake smile.

"Are you sure?"

He walked over to me and kissed my head. "Yes. We're sure. Jake is upstairs with Brayden if you want to go check on them."

"Sure. Okay."

I was confused as to what was going on and I didn't like it. After the barbeque was over and everyone left, my mom and dad summoned all of us in the living room. We all took our seats while my dad poured himself a drink.

"There's something I want to discuss with you. Do you remember me telling you about the woman I was involved with before your mother?"

"You mean the one that burnt down your Chicago office and the one Mom punched?" Collin asked.

"Yes, son. Her name is Ashlyn and she's back in New York. She's the woman you helped that day on the street."

I took in a sharp breath. "I didn't know she was out of jail."

"She got out three years ago and was living in Texas," my mom replied.

"Shit. I knew something was strange about her when she called me Connor."

"She's living here with her husband, whose company just transferred to New York. I'm not happy about this and it makes me sick. I want you all to stay away from her. If she approaches you, walk away. None of you are to have any contact with her at all. Do you understand me?" His tone was authoritative and stern.

"I don't even know what she looks like, Dad."

"Collin can tell you. Now I don't ever want to talk about this again. Understood?"

We all said yes at the same time. I looked over at my mom, whose eyes were filled with despair.

"The good thing is she's had years of therapy and she's married to a successful businessman. So honestly, I don't see her as a threat. But I want you all to be on guard," she spoke.

## Chapter 11
## Collin

I was sitting at my desk when the intercom rang. "Yes, Mom."

"Your next candidate is here for an interview."

I rolled my eyes. "Tell her to have a seat. I'll be with her shortly."

Interviewing these women was getting annoying. They were young, with only one thing on their minds. How did I know? The way they dressed and strutted into my office told me everything. They would sit down in the chair across from me, slightly lift up their skirts, and then cross their legs, sitting back in the chair in a seductive manner. One woman even had the nerve to wear a sheer white blouse with a black push-up bra underneath. The minute she unbuttoned her top three buttons, I booted her out of my office. These women obviously didn't care that I was married. I needed to find someone and fast. Work was piling up and my dad was keeping Laurinda very busy with his own projects. My mom tried to help out a few days a week, but the only thing she could do was answer the phones.

I got up from my desk and prepared myself for the person that was sitting outside my office. When I opened the door, I saw my mom talking to a guy. She was laughing.

"Collin, this is Ethan. He's here for the job interview." She gave me a wide grin.

Standing there in shock, I held out my hand. "Nice to meet you, Ethan."

We shook hands and I led him into my office. I turned and looked at my mom who was smiling at me.

"Please, have a seat," I spoke as I took my place behind my desk.

There was a knock at the door. "Come in."

My mom walked in and handed me Ethan's resume. "You forgot to grab this."

"Thanks, Mom." I smiled as I took it from her.

When she walked out and closed the door, Ethan spoke, "She's your mom?"

"Yeah. She's helping out until I find a replacement."

"Just in the few moments I spoke with her, I could tell she was a great woman."

"Thank you."

I leaned back in my chair and propped my ankle on my thigh, studying Ethan's resume. "You worked for Littlefield International?"

"Yes. I was the personal assistant to Matthew Convoy, assistant Vice President."

This was good. This was real good. "I see. They had to shut down a few months ago."

"Yeah. Poor accounting practices and too much embezzlement going on."

"That's what I heard. So tell me about yourself." I was liking him already. He reminded me of Mason when he was younger.

"I'm very organized, highly motivated, and I can multi-task like nobody's business."

"How come you haven't found a job yet, considering Littlefield shut down a few months ago?"

He looked down and began twiddling his thumbs. I could sense something was up and he became very nervous.

"It's okay, Ethan. You can tell me anything."

He looked up at me and took in a deep breath. "I had a short-term job after I left Littlefield, but it didn't work out."

"I don't see that on your resume. Did you get fired?"

"No. I quit. I didn't put it on my resume because it was a bad experience and the woman I worked for said that she would ruin me and she'd make it difficult for me to get another job."

Arching my eyebrow, I became intrigued. Leaning forward, I placed my hands on my desk. "Interesting. What happened? And I swear I won't hold it against you."

Uneasiness settled in as he began to tell me. "I took a job as the personal assistant to Kitty Chambers."

"Kitty Chambers, as in daughter of Gerald Chambers, CEO of Chamber Enterprises?"

"Yes. Now do you understand why I didn't want to mention this?"

"Please, go on. I can't stand that woman."

Instantly, he perked up. "Things started off pretty good and then she began to have me come to her home to do some work from there. After a while, she became very interested in me, if you know what I mean, and she asked me to do personal things for her."

"Such as?" I was desperate to know the juicy details.

"She wanted me to give her oral sex."

I chuckled as I leaned back in my chair. "I'm sorry. I don't mean to laugh, but I'm not surprised."

"In case you can't tell, I'm not into the female gender and I am in a very happy relationship with my boyfriend of two years. I told her this and she said she didn't care. All she wanted was oral sex, nothing else, and she wanted it at least three times a week. She even went so far as to schedule it. When I turned her down, she became irate and started making me do very menial tasks, which she called my punishment. The woman is a freak, Mr. Black."

I sat there and nodded my head. The rumors that I'd heard about her were now confirmed and I was taking great pleasure in it.

"I'm sorry she did that to you, and you have nothing to be ashamed of. You did the right thing by quitting."

"She told me that it will be a cold day in Hell before I get another job in the corporate world."

"Ethan, my man. I like you, and if you're interested, I would like you to come work for me and Black Enterprises. Your resume is impeccable and I can tell just by sitting and talking to you that you would be a great asset to me and this company. Can you start now? I really need my mom to go back to doing what she does best, and that's painting and being a mom."

His face lit up and a wide grin appeared across his face. "Thank you so much, Mr. Black. I would love to work for you, and yes, I can start now."

"Awesome. But one thing. Call me Collin."

He stood up from his chair as I extended my hand to him. "Thank you, Collin. Thank you again. You have no idea how much this means to me."

"You're welcome, and you have no idea how much this means to me."

Walking over to the door, I opened it and looked at my mom.

"Sorry, Mom, but your time's up here. You're free to leave. I've hired Ethan and he's agreed to start right now."

"That's wonderful, Collin. I knew he'd be perfect here." She smiled.

She got up from the desk and gave Ethan a light hug. Just a few moments of conversation and they'd already bonded.

"Congratulations, Ethan. If my son gives you any trouble, you call me. Here's my number."

"Mom. Stop it," I spoke as I narrowed my eyes at her.

She laughed as she placed her hand on my face and then headed to my dad's office.

"Come with me and I'll introduce you to my sister."

He followed me down the hall and I lightly tapped on Julia's door.

"Come in."

I walked in proudly and placed my hand on Ethan's shoulder. "Julia, I would like you to meet my new assistant, Ethan. Ethan, this is my sister, Julia Jensen," I spoke with a wide smile.

Julia got up from her desk and shook Ethan's hand. "It's nice to meet you, Ethan. I hope you enjoy working here."

"Thank you, Mrs. Jensen. I know I will."

"Please call me Julia. We aren't very formal around here."

"Ethan, why don't you go back to your desk and get acquainted with the space. I'll be there in a minute and introduce you to Laurinda, who will show you around."

He walked out of the office and Julia grabbed hold of my arm. "Oh my God, he reminds me of Mason."

"I know. Get this; he was a personal assistant to Kitty Chambers for a short while until she scheduled oral sex three times a week."

"Shut up!" She laughed.

"I'm dead serious. So now we know the truth about kinky Ms. Chambers."

"I'm happy you finally found your dream assistant."

"Me too." I kissed her forehead. "I'll talk to you later."

## Chapter 12
### Connor

As I leaned back in my office chair and stared at the pictures of my wife, children, and grandchild that graced my desk, I smiled at what a lucky man I was to have such a great life. That was until my cell phone rang and I took a call from my mother.

"Good morning, Mom," I cheerfully answered.

"Connor." Her voice was shaky.

I sat up in my chair. "Mom, what's wrong?"

"It's...it's… it's your father. He passed away this morning."

"What?" My heart started to ache and my mouth went dry. "Where are you?"

"I'm at the house."

"I'm on my way." *Click.*

I dialed Ellery.

"Hi, babe."

My lips could barely form the words. "Ellery, my father just passed away."

"WHAT?! Oh my God, Connor."

"I'm on my way to get you. We need to go to my mom. She's at the house."

"I'll be ready. I'm so sorry. I love you."

"I love you too."

I shut down my computer and sprang up from my chair. Walking out of the office, I headed to Collin's. "Laurinda, call Julia and tell her to get to Collin's office immediately. Also call Ralph and tell him I'm coming down."

"Sure thing, Connor," she said with concern.

My eyes were stinging from the tears that filled them. The minute I walked into Collin's office, he knew something was wrong.

"Dad, what is it?"

Julia came in right after me and shut the door. "What's going on, Dad?" she asked in a panic.

"Your grandfather passed away this morning."

"Oh no, Daddy." Julia wrapped her arms around me. Collin walked over and did the same. The three of us were locked in an embrace.

"I'm sorry, Dad," Collin whispered.

I tried to compose myself the best I could. "I need to go get your mom and we need to get over to Grandma's house right away."

"Do you want us to come with you?" Julia asked.

*A Forever Family*

"No. I need the two of you here. I'll call you when I know more." I kissed both of them. "I love you both very much."

"We love you too, Dad," they both replied.

I walked out and told Laurinda what had happened and that I'd be out of the office for a period of time.

*\* \* \* \**

Ellery was waiting outside the apartment building when Ralph pulled up. She flung open the door, climbed in, and wrapped her arms around me, holding me tight.

"I'm so sorry, Connor."

"I know, baby. I am too."

"Did Jenny say what happened?"

"No. I told her we'd be there as quick as possible. I need to be strong for her, Elle."

"You will be, baby. We all will be."

The limo pulled up in front of the house and I saw Cassidy standing at the door. The minute we got out, I ran to her and pulled her into an embrace. She was sobbing.

"I can't believe it, Connor. I can't believe he's gone."

"I know, sis. Where's Mom?"

"She's inside, sitting on the couch. I think she's in shock."

Walking inside, I made my way to the living room where I found my mom lying down.

"Connor," she spoke as she sat up.

Sitting down beside her, I pulled her into me and comforted her. "How did he die?"

"Heart attack. When he got out of bed this morning, he was irritable and not feeling well. He went into the bathroom and when he came out, he was clutching his chest and telling me to call 911. He passed away before they arrived. I screamed for the staff and Juan tried to give him CPR, but it was too late."

Ellery sat down on the other side of her and held her hand.

"Don't worry, Mom. We'll take care of everything."

"No need, Connor. Your father and I took care of all the arrangements a couple of years ago. Cassidy already called the funeral home. The viewing will take place the day after tomorrow and the funeral will be the next day. After that, all family and guests will come back here to the house for a luncheon."

I got up from the couch and walked over to the bar, pouring myself a scotch. First Denny and now my father. He hadn't been sick but maybe twice in his life.

"I want my family here for dinner tonight at six o'clock. Call the kids and make sure they cancel whatever plans they may have. This is a time when we all need to be together."

"I'll call them, Connor," Ellery spoke.

"I'll do it, baby." I pulled my phone from my pocket and did a three-way call with Julia and Collin.

"Hey, Dad."

"Hi, Dad."

"Your grandmother wants the family together for dinner tonight. Make sure you're here at six o'clock."

"How is she?" Julia asked.

"She's in shock right now."

"We'll be there, Dad. See you later," Collin spoke.

Finishing my drink, I walked back over to the couch and sat down.

"The newspapers have already been called and they're going to do a feature article on your father for tomorrow's paper." She got up and walked into the kitchen.

I looked at Ellery as she grabbed my hand and pressed her lips against it. "Are you okay?"

I sighed. "I don't know. Don't you think she looked a little robotic?"

"She's probably still in shock and it hasn't hit her yet."

"I guess." I put my arm around her and pulled her into me as I softly stroked her hair.

\* \* \* \*

"Damn it," I yelled as I struggled with my tie.

Ellery walked over and took my tie in her hands. "Here. Let me help you."

"I'm sorry, Elle."

"Don't apologize, sweetheart. This is very difficult for all of us."

*Sandi Lynn*

She tied my tie and reached up and kissed my lips.

I pulled her into an embrace and held her for a few moments. "I'm still mourning the loss of Denny and now my father." I broke our embrace and placed my hands on each side of her face. "I'm so happy to have you to go through this with. You're such a strong woman. I don't know what I'd do if I ever lost you."

Pursing her lips together, which gave way to a small smile, she spoke, "You're not going to lose me, Connor." Her lips softly brushed against mine. "We have to go or we're going to be late."

I put on my suitcoat, grabbed my wallet, and we climbed into the limo and headed to the funeral. After the service at the church, where many tears were shed, we went to the cemetery and watched as they lowered my father's casket into the ground. Sadness overwhelmed me as I held on tight to Ellery and my mother, while my children stood close, wiping the tears that fell from their eyes. As people walked up to us and gave their condolences, my eye caught the attention of a young man standing over by a tree a few feet away. He was the same man who I saw lurking around the funeral home yesterday and the same man I saw sitting in the back of the church this morning. He stared straight at me for a few moments and then turned and walked away. An uneasiness settled inside me and I didn't know why.

"Dad, what's wrong?" Collin asked as he came up next to me.

"See that guy over there walking away?"

"Yeah. Who is he?"

## *A Forever Family*

"I don't know. I saw him at the funeral home yesterday but he didn't talk to anyone. Just like he didn't talk to anyone here." I started to go after him. "Hey," I yelled as I got closer. He kept walking and didn't turn around. "Excuse me. Did you know my father?"

He stopped dead in his tracks and lowered his head. I stopped behind him and waited for him to turn around, but he didn't. He slowly turned his head to the side and, without looking at me, he spoke, "I met him once and I'm sorry for your loss. Now if you'll excuse me, I have somewhere I have to be." He continued to walk away.

"Connor, what are you doing? Come on; we have to get to your mom's house."

"I'm coming," I spoke as I continued to stare at the man who said he'd met my father once.

## Chapter 13
## Collin

People were scattered throughout the first level of the house and outside in the back where my grandmother had set up fancy tables, centerpieces, and tents throughout her massive backyard.

"Is this a funeral luncheon or a party?" Amelia asked as we looked around outside.

"My grandmother goes over the top with everything. Obviously, funeral luncheons aren't any different."

We walked around and visited with some of the guests that showed up, including Ashley and Ariel Braxton.

"Wow. Your grandmother sure knows how to put on a funeral luncheon." Ariel smiled as she gave me a light hug.

"We were just talking about that. I know I already sent you my congratulations, but now that you're here, I can give you a real one." I reached over and gave Ashley a hug. "You looked amazing on the cover of *Elle* Magazine."

"Thanks, Collin. It was a lot of fun."

"How's Alan doing?"

"We broke up a few weeks ago. I finally realized, after two years of my dad telling me what an asshole he was, that he was. I'm much happier now that he's out of my life."

"And what about you, Ariel? How's Brandon doing? I heard he just got traded and now he's playing for the LA Kings."

"Yes, and I couldn't be happier. He'll finally be back in L.A. where he belongs," she said with excitement.

The four of us talked for a while until I looked across the large, manicured yard and saw my dad sitting alone on a bench in the garden.

"Excuse me ladies. I need to go talk to my dad."

I made my way through the crowd of people and took a seat next to him.

"You okay, Dad?"

"Yeah, son. I just can't stop thinking about that guy at the funeral. I don't know why and I can't put my finger on it. There was something about him."

"I think you're obsessing too much over this. Maybe Grandpa helped him once and he wanted to pay his respects."

"Then why stand back in the crowd and not talk to anyone? Especially the family?"

"Maybe he's shy." I put my arm around him. "Come on, Dad. Let's get back to the luncheon. There's a whole lot of people to talk to."

He looked at me with a small smile. "You're right. Let's go."

We walked back to the house and my dad went to find my mom while I stopped and talked to my friend, Liam Wyatt.

"Liam, my friend. Thanks for coming." I gave him a light hug.

"So sorry about your grandfather."

"Thanks. I saw you at the funeral, but things have been a little crazy. I'm sorry I haven't had the chance to talk to you."

"Nah. No worries. Oliver and Delilah send their condolences. They'd be here if they could, but they took Sophie to Disney World. Hey, I know this is weird and all, but is something wrong with Hailey?"

"I don't know. Why?"

"I saw her in the house and she was acting weird. It's like she's on something."

"Julia said the same thing a few days ago. I don't know and, to be honest, I don't really care."

Amelia walked over to us, holding Brayden. "Hi, Liam." She smiled.

"Hi, Amelia. Congratulations on marrying this fool." He gave her a kiss on the cheek.

Laughter escaped her lips. "Thank you."

As we stood there talking, another good friend of ours walked over to us.

"Collin. We're so sorry for your loss," Max and Emma spoke as they both gave me a light hug.

"Thank you. I'm glad you guys are here. Hey there, Sarah." I smiled as she held out her arms and I took her from Max. "You are getting way too big too fast."

Amelia and Emma walked away and left us guys to talk.

"Any kids in your future?" Max asked.

"Someday. I would like to wait a couple of years."

"All my friends are off getting married and having babies, and I'm still trying to find that perfect girl." Liam pouted.

Max hooked his arm around him. "I just saw you the other night with that smoking hot chick at the restaurant."

Liam rolled his eyes. "Oh, she was hot and she knew it. She spent a majority of the night taking selfies and snap chatting. For a woman who was twenty-four, she acted like she was sixteen. I couldn't get her home fast enough."

Max and I chuckled and Sarah started to fuss and wanted to go back to Max. "I better go find Emma. Sarah's getting tired."

"Thanks again for coming. I appreciate it." I gave him a pat on the back.

"No problem, friend. I'll talk to you soon."

Liam and I talked for a few more minutes and then he had to get to the office and take care of a few things since Oliver was out of town. We said goodbye, and when I went to find Amelia, I found her talking to Hailey.

"Hey." I wrapped my arm around Amelia's waist.

"Hey." Hailey excused herself, and when she began to walk away, she dropped her purse and the contents spilled onto the floor. I bent down to help her pick it up and saw four prescription bottles full of pills and a small zippered baggie with a white powder in it.

"What are these?" I asked her as I picked up the bottles.

"Nothing." She grabbed them from my hands and nervously shoved everything back in her purse. "I'll talk to you guys later." She stood up and walked away.

"Maybe you should talk to her parents," Amelia spoke.

"It's none of our business, Amelia. Please. I don't want to discuss this again."

She wrapped her arms around me and pressed her cheek against my chest. "You always help people, Collin. That is one of the things I love most about you."

An anger began to brew inside of me. I was sick and tired of people trying to shove Hailey down my throat. I broke our embrace.

"Why can't you leave it alone?! I just lost my grandfather. Hailey is the last fucking person on this Earth I want to talk about!" I spoke in a raised voice.

I ran my hand through my hair and walked away to get some air. I stepped outside on the porch and sat down on the swing. I felt bad for raising my voice at my wife and, judging from the expression on her face, she was hurt. As I was sitting there thinking of a million ways to apologize to her, my mom came out and sat down next to me, taking hold of my hand.

"What's going on, Collin? I saw you storm out and Amelia standing in the middle of the room. Did you two have an argument?"

*A Forever Family*

I sighed. "No, Mom. It was more of me just being an insensitive asshole."

"Tell me what's going on. You know you can talk to me."

"Something's going on with Hailey and everyone is expecting me to fix it."

"What do you mean?"

"She's doing drugs, Mom."

"I see. Do you know that for sure?"

"Yes. Julia saw her doing coke in the bathroom at Peyton's birthday party and earlier, she dropped her purse. When I bent down to help her pick her things up, she had four bottles of pills and a baggie with coke in it. Julia and Amelia both want me to talk to her. It's none of my business. She's not my concern and I don't want to get involved."

She gave my hand a squeeze. "Between you and me, Peyton expressed her concern about Hailey a couple of days ago. She and Henry don't like this guy she's with. I know your history with Hailey isn't good, considering what you went through, but sometimes, we need to put the past behind us."

"So you're saying you put what happened with Ashlyn behind you?"

"God no! She's different. She's a psychotic bitch who tried to hurt my family. Hailey isn't like that. She's a good person, Collin. She's just lost right now."

I let out a sigh. "I hope she finds her way back someday, but I'm not going to be the one to show her the way."

"I understand."

Amelia walked out on the porch as my mom gave me a kiss on the cheek and went back inside the house. I held out my hand to her.

"I'm sorry, Amelia. I didn't mean to yell at you like I did."

She sat down beside me and laid her head on my shoulder. "I know you didn't. I shouldn't have pushed you like that. I love you."

"I love you too, baby."

## Chapter 14
### Connor

My mom decided to take a little weekend trip to Cape Cod with Cassidy, Ben, and Camden. She asked me if I would go through my dad's office and clean it out for her. She had already cleaned out his personal stuff, but the business was never her thing. She wanted everything out of there so she could turn his office into a sitting room. It was a Saturday morning and Ellery and I met Collin and Amelia for breakfast before we headed to the house. Collin drove himself, and after we finished breakfast, he drove us to the house while Ralph took the women into the city to do some shopping for the day.

"Thanks for coming and helping me with this, son."

"No problem, Dad."

While Collin was going through the filing cabinet, I cleaned out the bookshelf. As I pulled some books from the shelf, a white envelope fell from one of them and onto the floor. I bent down to pick it up and noticed it was filled with pictures. Sitting down in his chair, I opened the envelope and pulled out a picture of me and my brother Collin at the beach. It was taken the day he died. As I sat and stared at it, an overwhelming sadness washed over me.

"What is that, Dad?"

"A picture of me and your Uncle Collin." I handed the picture to him.

"Wow. Look at the two of you. I know he was your twin brother, but you almost look identical."

I gave him a small smile as I looked at the other photographs. There was one of our family and my mom holding Cassidy on her christening day.

"Dad, you dropped one," Collin spoke as he bent down and picked it up. He stared at it for a moment before handing it to me.

"Is this you or Aunt Cassidy?" he asked.

I took the photograph from his hand and looked at it in confusion. It was a picture of my father holding a baby in front of a house I didn't recognize. "It's neither of us. My father is a lot older in this picture."

"Then who is it? Is it Camden?"

"No." I looked through the remaining pictures. I stumbled across one of me and my dad at a banquet when he won the Businessman of the Year award. I held it next to the picture of him holding the baby and he looked the same. A sickness rose inside of me when my mind went to the place of something I didn't want to believe.

"Collin, I think my father had another child."

He laughed. "Dad, now you're getting crazy. Grandpa would never have cheated on Grandma."

"But he did, son, and I knew about it."

Shock swept over his face as he stood there and stared at me. "Who was she?"

"I don't know who she was. All I know is that he spent a month with her in the Caribbean while Black Enterprises was failing."

"Dad, I'm sorry."

I looked down at the desk and tried to pull open the bottom drawer. It was locked and I couldn't find the key.

"Go ask Juan for a screwdriver. I want to know what's in this bottom drawer."

A few moments later, Collin came back with a screwdriver. I shoved it in and busted the lock. When I opened the drawer, I found a file for the purchase of a house in Cherry Hill, New Jersey, dating back twenty-eight years ago. I gave the paper to Collin as I rummaged through the rest of the files.

"I didn't know Grandpa had a house in Cherry Hill."

"I didn't either. Let's go, son." I got up from the chair and walked out of the office.

"Where are we going?"

"To Cherry Hill, New Jersey."

\* \* \* \*

Collin pulled up to the curb of the house and we sat there a moment while I pulled out the picture of my father. It was the same house the picture was taken in front of. A small half brick, half vinyl-sided house with a bay window and a porch with a white railing. I swallowed hard as I got out of the Range Rover.

"Dad, what are you doing?"

"Hopefully getting some answers," I replied as I walked up the driveway and to the steps of the house.

"You can't just go up to someone's house like that." He followed behind me.

"I can and I will." I knocked on the door and waited a few moments. There was no answer, so I rang the doorbell. Still no answer.

"Fuck!" I ran my hand through my hair as I stepped off the porch and looked around.

"Can I help you with something?" an older woman asked as she was watering her flowers next door.

"I was wondering who lived here," I replied as I walked over to her.

"The Vines live there. Do you know them?"

"No. I don't think so." I handed her the picture. "Do you know this man and child?"

She looked at the photograph and then up at me. "You must be Mr. Black."

I was stunned and then startled when my phone rang. I pulled it from my pocket. It was Ellery. "Excuse me one moment. I need to take this." She nodded her head and continued to water her flowers.

"Hey, baby," I answered as I took a few steps away from the old woman.

"Hi, Connor. I was just checking in to see how things were going. We'll be heading to the house soon."

"Don't come to the house, Ellery. Collin and I aren't there."

"Where are you?"

"We're in Cherry Hill, New Jersey. It's a long story and I'll explain everything tonight. Just have Ralph drive you and Amelia back to the penthouse and Collin and I will be there later."

"Connor Black. What is going on?"

"Baby, please listen to me. I will explain everything later. I promise."

"You have me worried, Connor."

"There's no need to be worried. Collin and I are just checking out something we found in one of my father's files. I promise to tell you everything later, but now I have to go. I love you."

"I love you too. We'll be waiting at the penthouse for the two of you."

I sighed as I hit the end button and placed my phone back in my pocket. As I walked over to the older woman, she set her hose down and invited me and Collin inside.

"Please come inside for some iced tea and homemade cookies."

"Ma'am, I'm sorry but we—"

"Do you want your answers or not, Mr. Black?"

I gave her a small nod and swallowed hard as Collin and I followed her into the house.

"Have a seat in the living room and I'll get the iced tea and cookies." She smiled.

Collin and I took a seat on the floral couch. The room looked like it hadn't been updated in over thirty years.

"Here we go." The old lady smiled as she set a tray of cookies and iced tea down on the coffee table. "First off, we haven't properly met. I'm Flora Dunsworth." She extended her hand.

"I'm Connor Black and this is my son, Collin." I lightly shook her hand and Collin did the same.

Flora took a seat in the wing-backed chair that sat across from the couch. Collin reached over and grabbed a cookie from the tray.

"Oh my God, Flora, these are amazing!"

"Thank you, dear. They're my secret recipe. They've won all kinds of awards over the years."

I shot Collin a look because we weren't here to discuss how good her cookies were.

"Flora, you said you had answers for me. Did you know my father and this child?"

"Yes, I did. The woman who lived next door was Charlotte Oaks and that boy in the picture is her son, Lucas. We became very close."

I swallowed hard, finding it difficult to ask the next question. "Was Lucas my father's son?"

She pursed her lips together and looked down for a moment. She didn't need to say anything. The look on her face said it all.

"Yes. I had only met your father a couple of times. He didn't come around much due to the fact that, well, you know, he had another family."

My stomach twisted itself in knots and my heart raced at what Flora told me. I couldn't believe this shit. My father had a bastard son that he kept hidden all these years.

"They don't live there anymore?" Collin asked.

"No. Charlotte passed away about ten years ago and Lucas packed up his stuff and left. I felt sorry for Charlotte because she spent her life believing that your father would leave his family to be with her. I do remember an older gentleman who would come to the house to deliver some things to Charlotte over the years, but I can't seem to remember his name." She pressed her finger against her chin.

"Denny?"

"Ah, yes. Denny was his name. Nice man."

"How old is Lucas?" I asked as the sickness in my stomach intensified.

Flora sighed. "Let me think. You know my old brain isn't as sharp as it used to be. Lucas would be about twenty-eight now. Yes. That's right because he had just turned eighteen when Charlotte passed away."

"God, Dad. He isn't too much older than me and Julia."

I slowly shook my head, trying to absorb all the information Flora told me.

"May I ask how you found out about Charlotte and Lucas?"

"My father passed away recently, and as I was cleaning out his office, I found this picture and then the purchase agreement for the house."

"I'm so sorry for your loss."

"Thank you, but I'm not."

"Dad!" Collin exclaimed.

I got up from the couch and walked over to Flora, placing my hand on hers. "Thank you for your kindness and information. We have to get going."

"You're welcome, dear. I'm sorry you had to find out this way."

"Me too. Let's go, son."

"It was nice to meet you, Flora. Would you mind if I took some cookies home to my wife?"

I rolled my eyes.

"Of course you can. Let me go bag them up for you." She smiled.

## Chapter 15
### Connor

"You need to stop at the nearest bar. I need a drink," I said as Collin pulled away. "And really? You asked her for cookies?"

"Dad, they're amazing. Wait until you try one. Amelia will love them."

"I have a good mind to slap you right now. I just found out I have a brother who my father kept secret and all you're doing is thinking about cookies."

"Sorry, Dad. I'm just trying to lighten the mood. I know how rough this is on you. It is on me too. Are you going to tell Grandma?"

"No. She is to never find out about this. I will tell your mother and Julia and that's as far as it goes. No one else is to ever know."

He pulled into the parking lot of the Westminster Hotel.

"What are you doing?" I asked in irritation.

"You said you needed a drink. I'm sure there's a bar in this hotel."

"Good thinking, son."

We made our way inside the hotel and sat down at the bar inside the steakhouse restaurant. I ordered a double scotch and Collin ordered a whiskey sour. We sat in silence for a few moments as I thought about how to tell Ellery all of this. I pulled out my phone and sent a text message to Julia.

*"I need you and Jake to come by the penthouse later."*

*"Okay. Any special reason?"*

*"I just have something to talk to you and your mom about."*

*"Okay. See you later."*

"Julia said she and Jake will be by later." I took a large sip of my scotch.

"They're going to freak out. Like I am, Dad. I can't believe Grandpa."

"Yeah, well, I'm not surprised."

After I had another drink and Collin had coffee, we headed back to New York.

The elevator doors opened and Ellery and Amelia walked to the foyer to greet us.

"Are you going to tell me what's going on?" Ellery asked with concern as she wrapped her arms around me.

I kissed her head and held her tight. I didn't want to let go.

"What are those?" Amelia asked.

"Probably the best chocolate chip cookies in the world. Try one?"

*A Forever Family*

I reached over and lightly tapped the back of Collin's head.

"Ouch, Dad."

"Connor!" Ellery snapped.

"Where are Julia and Jake?"

"Upstairs putting Brayden down for a nap. He's really cranky," Ellery replied.

"Collin, go up and tell them to come downstairs."

I walked into the living room while Amelia and Ellery took seats.

"You are freaking me out, Connor. You better tell me what's going on right now!" Ellery said in a stern voice.

I pulled the picture from my pocket and handed it to her as Julia, Jake, and Collin walked in the room.

"I know that's your father, but who's the baby?"

I stood there and looked away. I was angry. So angry that I couldn't force the words out.

"That's Lucas. Dad's brother," Collin spoke.

"Your father doesn't have a brother, Collin."

"He does now."

I heard the gasps of my family, and when I looked at Ellery, she had a shocked look on her face.

"Connor?"

I took in a deep breath. "It's true. My father has another child and his name is Lucas. His mother's name was Charlotte and he bought them a house in Cherry Hill, New Jersey." I cleared my throat for it felt like my heart was trying to escape through it.

"How did you find this out? Did you talk to them?" Ellery asked.

"No. We talked to the neighbor, Flora. She invited us in for iced tea and these amazing cookies," Collin replied for me.

Julia got up and walked over to me and gave me a hug.

"I'm sorry, Daddy. I just can't believe this."

"You and me both, princess."

"Does your mother know about this?" Ellery asked.

"No, and we're going to keep it that way. Nobody outside this room is ever to find out about this."

"What about Cassidy?"

"Elle, I can't tell her. She'll be crushed and devastated. You know how close she and my father were."

"Secrets always come back to haunt you, Connor. You know that," she spoke.

"This is different because today never happened. Do you all understand me? We never went to Cherry Hill and we never heard of Charlotte or Lucas Oaks. Now if you'll excuse me, I'm going to go upstairs." As I began to walk away, I looked at Collin. "You are to forget about those damn cookies."

He frowned at me as I went upstairs and changed into my sweatpants and a t-shirt. I walked into the nursery and smiled at Brayden as he stared up at me and giggled. I picked him up and took him to my room, where we lay on the bed together. We both fell asleep.

I opened my eyes and Ellery was sitting on the edge of the bed, running her fingers softly through my hair.

"Did you have a nice nap?"

I stretched and looked over to see that Brayden was gone. "Yeah. Where's the baby?"

"Julia and Jake took him home. Everyone left a while ago. I didn't want to wake you." She leaned over and laid her head down on my chest. I wrapped my arm around her and softly caressed her back.

"I can't believe him, Ellery. I can't believe all of this."

"I know, baby. I can't either. Collin said that Lucas is about twenty-eight now. My God, he's not much older than our children."

"I think Lucas was the one I saw at the funeral. I told you I couldn't put my finger on it, but something was strange and it was the way he looked at me. He knew who I was."

She lifted her head and ran her hand down my cheek.

"You want to know what the worst part of all of it is? Denny knew. He knew about my father's affair and Lucas and he didn't tell me. He was my best friend, Elle." A tear started to form.

She got up and took my hand, pulling me into an upright position. "Come on; we're going to take a long, hot bath together and talk."

"I don't want to take a bath."

"Of course you do." She smiled as she lifted off her shirt and removed her bra.

"Fine. We can take a bath."

Ellery went into the bathroom and started the water while I got undressed. I climbed into the bubbly water first and she followed, snuggling into me with her back against my chest. The hot water felt good, but it felt even better holding her naked body in my arms. She knew this would relax me and she was right.

"I keep thinking about that letter Denny wrote me and how he said that I need to forgive my father as he grew older and all that shit about how people make mistakes and need to be forgiven. He was referring to Charlotte and Lucas because he knew that I'd eventually find out. Why didn't he tell me?" I ran my fingers up and down her arm.

"Because it wasn't his place to tell you. It was your father's place and you need to respect that."

"It still hurts, Elle."

"I know it does, baby." She kissed my arm. "Aren't you even curious about him?"

"No. I'm not. Not in the least. Life will go on as normal as if we never found this out. As for my dad's office, there's nothing I want in there and it can all be trashed, with the exception of the books that I'll have donated to the library. I'll call a company first thing in the morning. I'll be honest with you, Ellery, I don't think I'll ever be able to look at a picture of my father again."

She laid her head back and stared up at me, bringing her hand to my face. "We will get through this together, and I respect your decision whatever it may be. I love you, Connor."

"I love you too, baby. Let's get out of this tub. I want to make love to you all night."

She smiled as she got out of the tub, grabbed the oversized white towel, and wrapped it around both of us. I stood there in a warm embrace and became harder by the second as her beautiful body pressed against mine. Bringing my thumb to her cheek, I leaned in and brushed my lips against hers. Taking the towel from us, I dried her off before picking her up and carrying her to the bed, laying her down and hovering over her while my fingers dipped inside her. Soft moans escaped her lips as I explored her breast and took her hardened nipple between my teeth. Even after all these years and two kids later, her body was the most amazing and beautiful body in the world. She took great care of herself and so did I. Our sexual appetite for one another never diminished and it never would. I still wanted her every second of every day, and no other woman had ever caught my eye.

When I pressed my thumb down on her clit, she let out a moan and thrust her hips up, begging my fingers to go deeper inside of her.

"Come for me, baby. You're not getting my hard cock until you come for me."

Moving my thumb in circles against her clit and my fingers exploring every inch of her insides, her body shook and her legs tightened as she climaxed while calling out my name.

"That's my sweet girl." I smiled as I kissed her passionately.

I thrust myself inside of her and gasped. The warmth of her felt incredible as I moved in and out of her at a rapid pace. I didn't want to come yet, but she had me so hot that it was hard to hold back. I pulled out, rolled on my back, and pulled her on top of me.

"Ride me, baby. Make me come inside of you," I spoke with bated breath.

And that she did. She rode my cock fast and hard until we both climaxed at the same time. I thrust my hips up into her as I filled her insides. She threw her head back as I grabbed her breasts while she came down from her orgasm. Smiling, she leaned down and kissed me passionately before collapsing on top of me.

## Chapter 16
### Ellery

A month had passed since Connor's father passed away, and even though he seemed fine on the outside, I knew he was still torn up on the inside about the secret his father had kept. As I was getting ready for a family dinner at his mother's house, Connor walked into the bedroom and set his briefcase down on the bed.

"Hi, baby." He walked over to me and gave me a kiss on the lips.

"Hi. You need to hurry and change so we aren't late for your mom's dinner."

"I don't even want to go tonight. I don't know why she insists on having the family over. She's only going to be gone a month."

"She wants to see all of us one last time before she leaves. Is that so terrible?" I walked into the bathroom to check my makeup.

"Don't you think she's traveling a little too much since my father died? She doesn't even seem to be mourning him."

"Everyone handles death differently. Maybe she mourns in hiding."

"Who knows?" He sighed as he changed into a pair of khakis and a short-sleeved black polo. "Let's just get this night over with. I have some work to do when we get back home."

After finishing a nice dinner, we all gathered into the living room for a drink.

"Did you see the nice tribute *Forbes Magazine* did for your father?"

"No. I didn't," Connor replied in a stern voice.

"Let me go get it for you. It's a wonderful article."

"NO!" Connor spewed.

Even the mere mention of his father lately sent Connor into a rage. Nobody in the room said a word except for Cassidy.

"What the hell is your problem, Connor?"

"Nothing. I just don't want to see it." He walked over to the bar and poured himself a scotch.

He was going to lose it if they kept pushing. Collin and Julia glanced at me with concerned looks. They both saw what was coming too.

"It's a beautiful and respectful article, Connor. You should be proud that they would honor your father's memory."

"Maybe next time, Jenny," I spoke. "Connor, I'm not feeling well. I think we should go."

"Okay, Ellery." He set his glass down and walked over to me as I got up from the chair. He knew what I was doing and I could tell he was grateful.

"Your father would be very disappointed in you right now," his mother scowled.

Connor stepped dead in his tracks and I knew this was it. I braced myself for what was to come.

* * * *

## Connor

I balled my fist and pressed my lips together to keep from saying anything, but it didn't help. The anger of what my father had done and kept secret grew inside me every day. I turned around and looked at my mother as she stood there with her arms crossed.

"Disappointed? Him?"

"Dad, come on. Mom's not feeling well," Collin interrupted.

I held my hand up to him as I stared straight at my mother, my eyes burning into hers.

"Did the article go on to say what a respectable family man he was? How much he loved his wife and children? And how he'd be dearly missed?"

Her lips were twitching and I could see the anger grow within her eyes.

"Connor, that's enough. You're tired. We all are. We should go." Ellery grabbed my hand.

She was right. I needed to leave. We began heading to the foyer.

"How dare you disrespect your father that way!" she screamed.

I yanked my hand away from Ellery's and turned on my heels. "How dare I disrespect him? How dare he disrespect this family by having a love child with his mistress and keep him hidden away for the past twenty-eight years!" I yelled.

"What?!" Cassidy screamed. "Connor, that's enough!"

My mother looked down for a moment and didn't say a word. It was at that moment that I knew she had known about it. I stepped closer to her.

"You knew, didn't you?"

"Mom. What's Connor talking about?"

"We're going to go. Come on, Julia," Collin said. They all scurried out of the house.

My mother took a seat in her favorite wing-backed chair and refused to look at me. I paced around the room.

"Will someone tell me what the fuck is going on?" Cassidy yelled.

"Despite his shortcomings, he was a good man who provided well for his family," my mother spoke in a soft voice.

Cassidy walked over and knelt down in front of her. "So what Connor said is true? Daddy had another child?"

"Yes, Cass. We have a brother named Lucas and he's twenty-eight years old," I replied before my mother could even answer her.

My sister was hurt and tears started to fall down her face. Ellery walked over and wrapped her arm around her, leading her to the couch to sit down.

"Why didn't you ever tell us?" I asked calmly.

"Because it was nobody's business and I wasn't having this family's name ruined. Your father took care of the situation so no one would ever find out."

"He's my brother! Don't you think Cassidy and I had a right to know?"

She looked up at me with tears in her eyes. "How did you find out?"

"The day I came over to clean out his office for you. I first found a picture of him holding a baby outside a house. Then I found the purchase agreement for the house. Collin and I took a trip to Cherry Hill to find out what the hell was going on. That's when the neighbor next door told us everything. Lucas was at Dad's funeral. Did you know that? Do you even know him?"

She took in a sharp breath. "I saw him at the funeral and I spoke to him. I told him to leave and never come back. He had no business being there."

At this point, Cassidy was sobbing and Ellery was trying everything she could to comfort her.

"What the hell do you mean? That was his father! He had every right to be there!"

"Your father did what he had to do and made sure they were taken care of financially. That was the deal he made with Charlotte and she accepted. So now you know and it will never be discussed again. Now, if you'll excuse me, I'm going upstairs to bed. I'm leaving in a couple of days and I need my rest. Good night."

She left the room and I walked over to Cassidy and grabbed her hand. "I'm so sorry."

"Sorry? You should have told me the minute you found out."

"I know. But I didn't want you to hurt the way I was and still am. I was trying to protect you, sis."

"Protect me? I don't need protecting, Connor. I'm a big girl and I can handle what life throws me. I'm pissed off at you," she said as she got up from the couch. "I'm going home and I suggest you do the same. I'll talk to you when I calm the fuck down, but I don't know how long it'll take."

She left the house and I took a seat next to Ellery. She placed her arm around me and gave me a kiss on my cheek.

"I'm sorry, sweetheart."

"She pushed me, Elle. I had no choice but to say something."

"I know. It was bound to come out sooner or later. Let's go home, Connor."

## Chapter 17
## Collin

"So then it's settled." My mom smiled as she looked at me and Amelia. "We'll have your wedding reception at the beach house. I'll get the invitations ready."

"Thanks, Mom. We just want it to be casual and fun."

"We can discuss it more this weekend when we all go up there to celebrate Amelia's graduation."

I couldn't believe she was already graduating. I was so proud of her and all the things she had to overcome.

"If we're done here, Amelia and I have to go. We're meeting some friends at a club tonight to celebrate the end of Amelia's college years."

My mom stood up and gave us each a hug and kiss. "Have fun and I'll talk to you tomorrow. Ethan and I are having lunch." She smiled.

"Really, Mom? You're having lunch with my assistant?"

"Yes. Do you have a problem with that, Collin?" She raised her brow.

I sighed. "No, Mom. No problem."

"I didn't think so." She winked.

Amelia and I stepped into the elevator and went home to change and get ready for the club. When we arrived, our friends were already sitting at a table. We had a couple of drinks, talked, laughed, and had a great time. That was until I went up to the bar to get another drink and saw Hailey.

"Oh my God, Collin! It's so good to see you." She hugged me tight. "You know, since I've been back, we really haven't had a chance to talk. We should double date some time. I'd really like to get to know Amelia better."

She was overly excited and talking really fast. She was stoned out of her mind. Not only did her bizarre actions tell me, but so did her eyes. She was wearing a tank top and I noticed a large bruise on her arm.

"That's one nasty bruise," I commented as I pointed to it.

"Oh that. It's fine. I don't even know how it happened."

Marcus came up behind her and placed his hand on her waist. She flinched.

"Hey, Collin."

"Hey." I nodded.

"Come on, baby. We need to go now."

"But—"

"I said now!" he snapped.

"Think about that double date," she said as she walked away.

*A Forever Family*

I got our drinks and went back to the table. I was bothered by that encounter with Hailey and I knew she wasn't okay. Shit. I handed Amelia her drink and sat down, placing my hand on her shoulder and leaning into her.

"I just saw Hailey. She was stoned out of her mind."

"Of course she was. She has a problem."

"Something else was odd. When Marcus came up behind her and put his hand on her waist, she flinched. Almost as if she was scared."

"I don't know what to say, Collin. She's obviously troubled, so I think it's best we stay away from her."

"Yeah. Me too."

We continued the night with our friends, and as much as I tried to forget about my run in with Hailey, I couldn't.

That night, after making love, I held Amelia tightly against me.

"I know you're still thinking about Hailey."

I was stunned that she would even say something like that. "No I'm not. Why would you say that?"

"Because you're preoccupied and I know how much it bothered you to see her at the club."

"Amelia—"

She lifted her head and spoke before I could finish my sentence.

"It's okay, Collin. You can't help it and let me tell you why. It's in your nature. You help people. It's what you do. You and Hailey have history and, believe me, I'm not bothered by it at all. It's only natural that you're concerned about her no matter how much you try to deny it." She sat up and placed her hand on my chest. "If you want to talk to her and try to help her, then do it. But please stop trying to hide your concern. If you're doing it because you're worried about how I would feel, don't be. You're my husband and I love you no matter what you decide to do. I would feel horrible if something happened to her and you didn't at least try to talk to her."

I stared into her beautiful eyes and placed my hand on her cheek. "You're an amazing woman, Amelia Black, and I'm pretty sure I just fell more in love with you at this moment, which I didn't think was possible."

She smiled as she leaned down and softly brushed her lips against mine. "I love you too and I know you'll do what's right. Now we have to get some sleep. Six o'clock will be here sooner than we think. Good night, my husband."

"Good night, my wife. You owe me shower sex in the morning."

She softly laughed as she snuggled back into me and laid her head down on my chest.

\* \* \* \*

I was sitting in my office when my dad walked in, threw a file on my desk, and sat down.

"Congratulations on sealing the Lupinski deal. I couldn't have done it better myself."

"Thanks, Dad. It was a piece of cake." I smiled as I leaned back in my chair. "I was thinking about taking a trip out to California to see Diana and Jacob."

"Good idea. I think you should. It's been a while. When were you thinking about going?"

"Maybe after we get back from The Hamptons. Amelia's clinicals are over and she doesn't start her job as a full-time RN for two weeks."

My intercom rang. "Yeah, Ethan?"

"There's a call on line one for you, Collin." He cleared his throat. "It's Ms. Chambers."

The corners of my mouth curved up into a smile as I looked at my dad. "Thank you, Ethan, and I'm sorry you had to take that call."

I pressed line one and kept it on speakerphone. "Hello, Kitty, how are you?"

"Pissed as hell, Collin," she snapped.

I rolled my eyes and sighed. "I suppose you heard about Lupinski."

"Yes, I did, and how sneaky of you to steal him and that deal out from under me. I've been trying to call your father, but he won't return my calls."

"That's because my father is a very busy man and has nothing to do with this. What were you planning on doing? Tattling on me? Listen, Kitty. Lupinski saw a better opportunity with Black Enterprises than he did with Chambers Enterprises. All is fair in business negotiations."

"There is no way you could have offered him a better deal than what I did. If you did, then you better be prepared to lose your ass on that deal."

"I'm not losing anything, Kitty. The deal was fair. Lupinski knew it and he accepted. I looked at the bigger picture."

"You're a snake, Black, and this isn't over."

"I've been called worse. By the way, I love my new assistant, Ethan." I sat up and leaned closer to the speaker. "This is over, Kitty, and let me warn you. If you so much as start anything, your little kinky secrets and sexual harassment with your employees will be exposed. I don't think Daddy would like to hear the things his princess does behind closed doors and during office hours. Good bye, Kitty."

My dad snickered. "Ah. You truly are a chip off the old block and I couldn't be prouder, son."

"Thanks, Dad. Now about that vacation to California…"

"Consider it a business trip. I want you to go to the gallery and check everything out. I'll have the plane ready for Monday. Just let me know a time."

"Since we're coming back from The Hamptons Sunday night, Amelia and I will probably want to leave around noon if that's okay?"

"Noon it is." He got up from his chair. "I'll call the pilot now and have it put on the manifest."

I couldn't wait to tell Amelia we were going to California and I was beyond excited to see Jacob again.

## Chapter 18
### Ellery

I opened my eyes as the sun filtered through the crack of the closed curtains. I rolled over and Connor's side of the bed was empty. I climbed out, slipped on my robe, and followed the aroma of freshly brewed coffee to the kitchen.

"Good morning, baby." He smiled when I walked in.

"Good morning. Why didn't you wake me up?" I walked over and gave him a kiss.

"You were sleeping so peacefully that I didn't want to disturb you. We had a long night last night between Amelia's graduation and then coming straight here to the beach house."

"You're sweet, darling, but we have so much to do for the party tonight."

"Don't worry. You already have everything covered." He placed his hands on my hips. "There's something I want to discuss with you."

"Can I have some coffee first?" I smiled.

"Of course you can. Go sit down and I'll bring you a cup."

I watched him as he reached up into the cupboard and took down a mug. He seemed to be doing better since his confrontation with his mother and he and Cassidy had worked things out. He set the coffee cup in front of me and kissed the top of my head. Taking a seat next to mine, he held his cup in his hand and looked at me.

"I'm thinking that maybe it's time to retire and hand the company over to Collin."

"What? You said you were going to wait a couple of years," I spoke in surprise.

"I know, but Collin has more than proven himself and I know that between him and Julia, I don't have to worry. We can start traveling more and seeing the places we always wanted to see."

"I love the idea, Connor, but—"

He took hold of my hand. "I know what you're thinking, Elle. You're worried about Brayden. But don't be. We won't take long vacations and my thought is that it's best to do this now before Julia and Jake have another baby. Plus, don't forget, Collin and Amelia may surprise us one day."

"True."

"At that point, we could just take care of our grandchildren while our own children go off to work and run my company."

I set my cup down and leaned into him. "I love the idea. When were you planning on handing the company over?"

"I was thinking within the next three months. I have Lou working on some things."

*A Forever Family*

There was a knock at the door and Connor got up to answer it. The thought of him retiring excited me. We'd been talking about this moment since the day the children were born. Being with him every day, traveling to the most exotic places, and not having to worry about Black Enterprises was a dream. I'd miss my children terribly when we were gone, but we raised them, and now that they had families of their own, it was time for me and Connor to spend some time alone without any worries.

\* \* \* \*

## Collin

My parents threw a huge graduation party for Amelia, and I couldn't have been happier. It was something I wanted to do myself for her, but my mom told me not to be silly and that she would take care of it. She loved the control and I couldn't fault her for it, especially since I got married in Vegas without them.

"Hey, Jake, do you know where Julia is?"

"Yeah. She's down by the water with Brayden. Speaking of the water, how about a little surfing tomorrow morning before we leave?"

"Sounds good, bro."

I walked down to the beach and saw Julia bent over, holding Brayden so his feet were getting wet by the water.

"He seems to love that." I smiled as I walked up next to her.

"He does. He's going to love it here just like we do. Think about it, Collin, when I have more kids and you and Amelia start a family, we can create the same memories here that Mom and Dad did for us."

"We sure can. I'm looking forward to it. I wanted to talk to you."

"What's up?"

"When me and Amelia were at the club last week, I ran into Hailey and she was stoned out of her mind. She was saying all sorts of weird shit like how she wants to get to know Amelia better and how we should double date. I may be going out on a limb here, but I think Marcus is hurting her physically."

She turned her head and narrowed her eyes at me. "Why do you think that?"

"She had a large bruise on her arm and she said she didn't know how it happened."

"So? I get bruises all the time and I don't know where they came from." She handed me Brayden and I continued to soak his feet in the water.

"When he walked up to her and placed his hands on her hips, she flinched."

"Maybe she was surprised and caught off guard."

"Nah. I saw the look of fear in her eyes. When he said they were leaving, she tried to tell him no and he yelled at her."

"Maybe he doesn't like her talking to her ex-boyfriend," Julia spoke.

"Whatever. She approached me. My point is, I need to put the past aside and talk to her in private about her problem. If she keeps going down this road, something's going to happen to her."

## A Forever Family

"I agree and I'm thrilled you want to finally talk to her about it, but people can't be saved unless they want to be."

"I know. But I'd feel a lot better if I at least tried. I just don't understand what happened to her. Peyton and Henry are amazing and loving parents."

"Sometimes people just fall off the right path."

Brayden started to cry. "I think this little dude has had enough of the water. Come on, buddy, let's go back to the house and dry off those feet."

Julia hooked her arm around me and we walked back to the party. Amelia was off talking to her college friends and I saw Peyton at the bar, getting a drink.

"Hi, Peyton. Do you have a minute?"

"Sure, sweetie. What's up?"

"How's Hailey doing?"

She took a sip of her drink and sighed. "May I ask why you're asking?"

"The few times I saw her, she doesn't seem herself and I'm concerned."

We slowly started to walk out of the tent. "Henry and I have said the same thing. We think she's doing drugs and we don't know what to do. We don't like that Marcus guy she's with at all. I'm really worried about my little girl, Collin. We've tried to talk to her, but she shuts down and tells us that she's fine and that she's really happy."

"I was thinking about talking to her. Maybe asking her to go to lunch one day."

"I think she would like that. I know it's not easy for you, considering the history you two have, but I think she would listen to you."

"Okay. Then as soon as I get back from California, I'll have a talk with her."

Peyton wrapped her arm around me and gave me a hug. "Thank you, Collin. You have no idea how much this means to me."

My dad and I stood at the bar and did a few shots. Okay, we did more than a few and were pretty drunk. So drunk that after the party ended and everyone left, Amelia had to hold me up while we walked home and my mom had to help my dad into the house. We had a great time, though, and the best was yet to come for our wedding reception.

"I'll bring you the cocktail in the morning," I heard my mom say to Amelia.

"Thanks, Mom. He's going to need it."

"So is his father."

"I'm not drinking that shit," my father and I both said at the same time as we attempted to high five each other and missed.

* * * *

"Drink up, sleepy head," I heard a voice say. I opened one eye and saw Amelia standing over me with a glass in her hand.

I moaned and rolled over.

"Oh no you don't. Jake is waiting for you to go surfing, so you better drink this and not disappoint him. Between this cocktail and the ocean water, you'll feel better."

I turned on my back, forced myself to sit up, and took the glass from her, chugging it down as fast as I could. God, I hated this shit. I always had and every time I was hungover, my mom shoved it down my throat. Now I had my wife doing the same thing.

"Good boy. Now get up and put your wetsuit on." She smiled as she kissed my forehead.

I unsteadily climbed out of bed, brushed my teeth, and pulled on my wetsuit. My head was thumping and the last thing I wanted to do was to go surfing. I grabbed my surfboard and we walked down the beach to my parents' house. My dad and Jake were sitting on the patio with sour looks on their faces and a cup of coffee in their hands.

"Morning." I set my surfboard down and took a seat next to Jake. "Sorry I'm late."

He put up his hand. "No, please. Don't apologize. I just got up a few minutes ago myself."

He looked just as hungover as I did and so did my dad.

"Rough night for us," I spoke.

Both of them slowly nodded their heads. "Yep. It sure was."

"Did you drink it?" I asked them both.

"Had no choice," they replied in unison.

After about an hour of sitting there, quietly talking and trying to feel better, Jake and I grabbed our boards and hit the water.

\* \* \* \*

## Connor

Standing at the edge of the path between the beach house and the beach, I stared at my family as they were enjoying the water, sun, and sand. It seemed like yesterday I was showing Ellery this house after our wedding.

"What are you doing?" Ellery asked as she wrapped her arm around my waist.

"Just watching our children down there having fun. I was just thinking about how it seemed like yesterday when I brought you here for the first time."

She laid her head on my shoulder. "It sure does. This house holds a lot of wonderful memories. Before you know it, Brayden will be running up and down that beach all by himself and Jake will be teaching him how to surf."

Julia turned around and waved to us. "Why are you two just standing up there? Get down here and enjoy your last day with us!"

I took Ellery's hand and we walked down to where Julia and Amelia were sitting. I bent down and picked up Julia.

"Daddy! What are you doing?"

"Do you remember when I used to do this?"

"Daddy, put me down. Don't you dare take me into the water!"

"Come on, princess. Just like old times," I said as I walked in the water with her screaming and threw her.

Once she surfaced, she rubbed the water from her eyes and came after me, just like she used to when she was a kid. We played around in the water, splashing and trying to pull each other under. Jake and Collin abandoned their surfboards and joined us. Amelia and Ellery stepped to the shoreline and Collin grabbed Amelia and threw her in the water. Ellery looked at me and shook her head because she knew I was coming for her.

"I have your grandson, Connor. Don't you dare. I swear to God, Connor," she screamed as Jake grabbed Brayden and I picked up Ellery, carrying her into the water.

"You'll pay for that, Connor!" she yelled. "No more sex for you!"

"Mom. Gross. Stop it!" Collin yelled as I laughed.

I swam out to her and placed my hands on her face. "You couldn't withhold sex from me no matter how hard you tried."

"You're right. But I knew it would make the kids cringe." She softly kissed my lips.

And that was how our day was spent in The Hamptons, at the beach house. Playing in the water, reminiscing about old times, and just plain having fun as a family. A family with a bond so strong, nothing could ever break it.

We had one last barbeque and then cleaned up and headed back to the city.

"Julia, why don't you let us take Brayden in our car? It'll give you and Jake a chance to be alone and talk for a while."

"Thanks, Daddy. I think we'll take you up on that offer."

Just as we loaded both cars, Collin and Amelia pulled up to the curb. "You guys ready to head back?"

"We sure are." Julia smiled as she climbed in the car.

I pulled out first, then Julia and Jake pulled out, and Collin followed behind.

## Chapter 19
## Collin

I took Amelia's hand and brought it up to my lips. We had an amazing weekend and the week was only going to get better leaving for California.

"Are you excited to go to California?"

"I'm very excited. You didn't tell Jacob we were coming, did you?"

"No. I just told Diana and she said she wouldn't tell him. We want to surprise him. It'll be great to see them again. Also, we're going to go out with Ashley and Ariel while we're there."

"And don't forget about Mason and Landon." She smiled.

"How could I? Mason's been texting me nonstop with excitement. He and Landon are taking us out to celebrate your graduation."

"Maybe we need two weeks in California." She laughed.

So far, the drive home was smooth. It was night and darkness had settled in, but traffic was light. Julia and Jake were in front of us and my parents were nowhere to be seen. I pulled out my phone and dialed my dad.

"Yes, Collin."

"Where are you?"

"I decided to take a different route than usual. I want to see if it's any faster."

"And what time does the GPS say you'll be arriving home?" I asked with a cocky attitude.

"Fifty-three minutes."

"I see. We should be pulling in at the same time. See you in fifty-two minutes, Dad."

I heard him sigh as he ended the call. We continued our drive and up ahead was an intersection about twenty minutes from home. One of our favorite songs came on the radio and I turned it up and started singing to Amelia. I looked at her for a split second and ran my thumb down her cheek. Suddenly, she screamed.

"Collin, oh my God! STOP!"

I looked ahead and everything went into slow motion. I slammed on the brakes as I watched a truck slam into Julia and Jake's car as they went through the intersection, sending it into another car before rolling over. The crash was a sound I'd never forget. The squealing of the tires and the thumping sound of the car hitting the cement as it rolled over. My heart was pounding and Amelia was crying. I swung open the door as I screamed Julia's and Jake's names. Cars stopped and people got out to see what had happened. I ran over to the car and got down on the ground, Julia was lying there with tears streaming down her face and blood pouring from her forehead. I looked over at Jake and he was unconscious.

*A Forever Family*

"FUCK!" I yelled. "Julia, close your eyes tight."

Amelia and I ran over to Jake's side and I told her to stand back as I kicked the window as hard as I could, causing it to shatter. Amelia pushed me out of the way and checked Jake's pulse.

"He's alive. Thank God. He's alive."

I reached in and over Jake, taking hold of Julia's hand, trying to calm her down.

"Julia. You're going to be okay. The ambulance is on its way. Just hold on."

"I can't move, Collin," she said in a weak voice.

"Don't try to move, Julia. It's important that you don't move."

"Jake!" she screamed.

"Jake is going to be fine. He's alive and so are you." Tears were streaming rapidly down my face as I held her hand.

"My baby. Where's my baby?"

"Brayden is safe. He's with Mom and Dad. Amelia, call my parents and tell them what happened."

Before long, the ambulance arrived and attended to Julia and Jake quickly. I got up and hugged Amelia tightly as she sobbed into my shoulder. We both were shaking uncontrollably. A police officer walked over to us and asked us what happened.

"We were driving behind them and the light was green. Out of nowhere, that truck just slammed into them."

"That driver is drunk and we're taking him into custody. Thank you for your statement."

The paramedics got Jake and Julia out of the car and placed them on the stretchers.

"This one's in bad shape. We need to get her to the hospital stat. Call the ER and tell them to have a team ready and that we're on our way." They put her in the ambulance. I needed to be with her.

As the other paramedic was taking Jake's vitals, he started to regain consciousness and screamed Julia's name.

"She's going to be okay, Jake. You both are," I said as I held his hand. He looked at me as tears filled his eyes. I wanted to break down right then and there, but I couldn't. I needed to be strong for him and for my sister. "Amelia, stay with Jake. I'm going to ride to the hospital with my sister. Can you drive to the hospital?"

"Yes. Just go. I'll be fine."

I gave her a kiss and climbed in the ambulance with Julia as they shut the doors and took off, sounding their lights and getting us to the hospital as fast as they could.

* * * *

# Julia

The sound of the crash. The lights fading into the distance and the excruciating pain that radiated through my body was unbearable. I lay on the stretcher, fighting for my life as my brother cried and held my hand. He kept telling me that everything was going to be okay. But I wasn't so sure. Sounds were fading in and out and dizziness overtook me. Before I knew it, I was being raced down the hallway of the hospital. A team of doctors waited for me inside the room that would determine my fate. I was alone in a room full of strangers who were trying to help me. As they cut off my clothes, I heard one of the doctors say I had internal bleeding and they needed to get me to surgery stat. I looked up as a nurse was cleaning the wound on my forehead.

"You're going to be just fine, Julia. Hang in there, sweetie." She gently smiled.

Once again, I was being raced down the hallway and into the surgical room where they injected me with a needle and put a mask over my face. Silence fell upon my ears as darkness overtook my eyes.

"You're going to be okay, kid," I heard a familiar voice say.

I turned around and I was standing in the hallway outside the surgical room. I looked around for the familiar voice and, when I turned my head, Denny was standing in front of me.

"Denny." I smiled. "Where am I?"

"You're in limbo right now, but soon enough, you'll be waking up. It's not your time, Julia. You still have your whole life ahead of you."

"How do you know?"

"Trust me. I know."

He looked so good and so happy. "Are you okay?" I asked him.

"I'm fine. Better than I ever had been. Do me a favor and tell your old man to stop being stubborn. Tell him he knows the right thing to do and that forgiveness always prevails. Everything happens for a reason, Julia. The big guy upstairs makes things that way. I have to go now. You'll be waking up soon. Take care of your family and kiss that baby boy of yours for me."

As he started to walk down the hallway, he slowly began to disappear in the distance. "Denny, wait!" I screamed. A force so strong held me back and everything went black.

## Chapter 20
### Connor

We met Collin and Amelia in the waiting room. Ellery was hysterical as she hugged him.

"She's in surgery, Mom. We haven't heard anything yet."

I hugged Amelia tightly as she broke down and cried. After both women started to settle down, I hugged Collin like he was the last person on earth.

"What the fuck happened?"

"A drunk driver ran a red light at the intersection and hit Julia and Jake. Julia's side was hit. Dad, I'll never forget what I saw." He started to sob in my arms.

We waited for what seemed like eternity before the doctor came into the waiting room. "Mr. and Mrs. Black?" the surgeon asked.

"Yes," I answered as Ellery held on to me.

"I'm Dr. Perry, the surgeon who worked on your daughter, Julia. She has sustained some injuries and we had to stop some internal bleeding in her abdomen. Unfortunately, her kidneys took the impact of the accident and we had to remove one that was completely severed."

Ellery was about to collapse as Collin grabbed her from behind. "Sit down, Mom."

"If you're not aware, you can lead a completely normal life with one kidney, however, the second kidney was also damaged and I repaired as much as I could. I have a nephrologist coming in to talk to Julia in the morning about the next step."

"When can we see her?"

"She'll be waking up from the surgery soon. I will warn you that she will be in a lot of pain, but the nurses will have her on pain medication through her IV. We put her in a room with her husband. He's fine. Just some bruises, but we want to keep him here overnight for observation."

"Thank you, Dr. Perry."

I sat down next to Ellery and held her. "She's going to be just fine, baby. Our little girl is going to be okay."

"She has one kidney, Connor, and the other is damaged. I don't call that fine!" she yelled.

"She's alive and that's all that matters. We'll deal with the rest later."

A nurse walked in and led us to Julia and Jake's room. Standing in the doorway, an overwhelming fear took over me and I found it difficult to step inside the room. Ellery ran over to Julia's bedside and began to cry. Jake stared at me from his bed and I could see the tears spring to his eyes. I walked over to him and grabbed his hand.

*A Forever Family*

"I'm so sorry." He began to cry.

"It's not your fault. I'm just glad you're both alive."

"She's going to be okay, right?"

"Yes, son. She's going to be okay." I gave his hand a gentle squeeze and Collin and Amelia walked over.

I looked at my princess and my heart started to race. Thinking of how we could have lost her terrified me. I placed my hands on Ellery's shoulders. She let go of Julia's hand and walked over to Jake. I sat down on the edge of the bed and held her hand, holding back the tears that so desperately wanted to escape. I needed to stay strong for Ellery and for Jake. I buried my face in my daughter's arm and said a silent prayer.

"Daddy," I heard a soft whisper.

I lifted my head and Julia was staring at me. "What happened?"

"You were in an accident, princess, but you're going to be just fine."

Ellery ran over to the other side of the bed and gave her a light hug. "My baby," she cried.

"Where's Jake?"

"I'm right here, sweetheart." He smiled.

Collin and Amelia gave us some time with Julia before they walked over to see her.

"Thank you," Julia whispered to Collin. "You were there holding my hand and telling me that I was going to be okay."

"You would have done the same for me." He smiled at her.

"Where's my baby?"

"Brayden is with Peyton and Henry. Don't worry about him. He's fine."

Julia started to cry. "What if he was in the car with us?"

I leaned over and lightly gripped her shoulders. "Princess, he wasn't and that's all that matters."

"Why am I in so much pain? My back and my stomach hurt so bad."

"Collin, go get the nurse," I spoke.

Ellery leaned down and pressed her lips against Julia's hand. Telling her what had happened to her was going to be one of the hardest things I ever had to do. I swallowed hard and took in a deep breath.

"Julia, your kidneys took the impact of the crash. The doctors had to remove one of them."

Shock splayed over her face as tears ran down her cheeks. "I only have one kidney?"

"Yes, princess." I gulped. "A nephrologist will be here in the morning to talk to you about your other kidney. It was also damaged but not as severe as the other one."

She turned her head and looked at Jake. "Oh my God," she sobbed.

The nurse walked into the room and saw how upset Julia was. "I'm going to give her a sedative. She needs her rest tonight. So say goodbye and you can come back in the morning."

"There is no way I'm leaving my daughter!" Ellery snapped as she stood up from the chair.

"Mom, it's okay. I want to be alone with my husband. You and Daddy go home and get some rest. I'll see you tomorrow."

"Julia!"

"Mom, please. I need to be alone with Jake."

We kissed Julia and Jake goodbye and the four of us walked out of the room, preparing ourselves for what the nephrologist would tell us in the morning. Somehow, I had a feeling it wasn't going to be good.

\* \* \* \*

## Ellery

It was almost midnight when we stopped by Peyton and Henry's apartment to pick up Brayden. We told them everything that had happened and what the doctor said. Henry said that he'd stop by Julia's room in the morning and look at her chart. Connor tried to get hold of Jake's parents, but they were vacationing in Europe. He didn't want to tell them on a voice message what had happened, so he just said to call him when they had a chance. As we were driving back to the penthouse, I pulled out my phone and dialed Mason.

"Hello, sweet cheeks. To what do I owe the pleasure of speaking to you today?" he spoke in a cheerful voice.

My voice was shaky and I began to cry. "Can you come to New York right away? We need you."

"Elle, what happened?"

"Julia and Jake were in a bad accident and we need you to help with Brayden."

"Oh my God. Are they okay?"

"Julia has some issues. Please, Mason. I need you."

"I'm on the next flight out, Elle. Don't worry. Is Brayden at the penthouse with you?"

"Yes. We're taking him there now."

"Okay. I'm on my way."

We finally arrived home and Connor carefully laid Brayden down in his crib. Connor and I changed out of our clothes quickly and into our pajamas. We were both exhausted as I snuggled up against him.

"She's going to be just fine, baby."

"I hope so. Because if she's not, I don't know what I'll do." I kissed his bare chest as he kissed the top of my head.

The next morning, my eyes flew open and I was still wrapped around Connor's body. I looked at the clock and it read seven a.m.

"Connor, wake up. Brayden never woke up this morning. How did we sleep so late?"

"Ellery, I'm sure he's tired."

I jumped out of bed, threw on my robe, and ran down to his room. He wasn't in his crib, but I could smell the aroma of coffee infiltrating the penthouse. Only one person made a special blend of coffee that smelled like that. I walked down the stairs and into the kitchen where Mason was feeding Brayden his oatmeal.

"When did you get here?" I asked with a sigh of relief as I walked over and kissed him.

"I got in about two hours ago."

I poured a cup of coffee, said good morning to my grandson, then sat down and let the tears fall once again.

Mason put his arm around me. "Aw, Elle, don't. Our princess is going to be okay."

"He's right, baby. Julia is going to be fine," Connor spoke as he walked into the kitchen.

"Hello there, handsome daddy."

"Thanks for coming so quickly, Mason." Connor gave him a light hug.

"Anything for my favorite family. You know I'm always here for you."

Connor took Brayden from his bouncy seat and held him close, kissing the top of his head. I couldn't stop thinking about how he could have lost his parents. The thought consumed me as my tears flooded my face. Mason gripped my shoulders.

"Listen to me, Elle. You aren't going to do this anymore. This isn't like you. You're one of the strongest women I know and for you to keep breaking down like this is unacceptable. I'm sure you had your fill of tears last night and that's fine. But now, you need to dry them up because you need to be strong for Julia. Do you want her to see you fall apart? She was in a horrific accident and the last thing she needs is her mother losing it. She's alive, Elle, and that's all that matters. All the rest will fall into place. Whatever she may face or what's yet to come, you have to be strong for her."

"He's right, baby. Listen to him. Julia needs us more than ever right now and we can't let her down. We better go get ready. Mason, can you bring Brayden by the hospital later so Julia and Jake can see him? I'll send Ralph to drive you."

"Of course I will."

I went upstairs, showered, and got dressed. Jake's parents had called Connor back and wanted to get on the next flight home. He told them that everyone was okay and to finish their vacation, not to worry, and that he'd keep them updated every day. I was a nervous wreck on the way to the hospital with the fear of what bad news about Julia was to come.

## Chapter 21
### Julia

I missed my baby and I wanted to hold him. Jake had climbed in bed with me last night and carefully held me. I was still in a lot of pain and had nightmares about the accident. I hadn't told my dad yet about Denny. In fact, I didn't even tell Jake. If I did, people would think I was crazy. But I wasn't. It was real. He was real and he had spoken to me. I tried to wrap my head around the things he said about my dad. I didn't understand, and if I told my dad, he wouldn't understand either. For now, I planned on keeping this my little secret.

"I miss Brayden, Jake."

"I do too, sweetheart. I'm being released today so I'll bring him up to see you."

My mom and dad walked into the room with Collin and Amelia following behind. My mom looked as if she'd been crying.

"Good morning, my sweet girl." She put on a brave smile as she leaned over and kissed me.

"Good morning, Mom. Dad. Collin. Amelia."

My dad leaned over me, placing his hand on my head. "How are you feeling, princess?"

"Not real good. I'm so tired and in pain. How's Brayden?"

"Brayden is fine, Julia," my mom spoke as she took hold of my hand. "Mason flew in and is taking care of him. He's bringing him up later."

A small smile escaped my lips. Knowing that Mason was here eased my mind.

"Hey, sis." Collin smiled as he kissed my cheek. "Did you sleep okay?"

"I did once Jake climbed in bed with me. You're supposed to be in California."

"Nah. We postponed it. There's no way I was leaving when you're stuck in here."

The door opened and a tall, older gentleman in a white coat and black-rimmed glasses stepped in.

"Good morning, Julia. I'm Dr. Benson and I'm a nephrologist."

"Hi, Dr. Benson." I introduced him to my family.

"I looked over your chart and spoke with Dr. Perry. I also got the results back of your bloodwork from this morning. Your other kidney isn't functioning like we hoped it would. Now, it is still early, so we're going to carefully monitor you over the next week to see if there's any improvement."

Tears filled my eyes and breathing became difficult.

"And if there is no improvement, doctor?" Jake spoke.

*A Forever Family*

"Then you have two options: A kidney transplant or dialysis, which you'd be on the rest of your life. Considering your age, I think a transplant would be the best option. But like I said, we won't fully know until about a week."

"When can I go home?" I asked.

"Not for a few days. I'll keep monitoring your bloodwork and ultrasound scans that you'll be having. It was nice to meet you all. Take care, Julia." And, just like that, he walked out of the room.

I lay there in shock, Jake gripping my hand tightly and trying to hold back the tears. My mom and dad staring at me with somber looks on their faces and Collin and Amelia looking down. Nobody knew what to say. This was not the news I was hoping for. Suddenly, my mom perked up and walked over to me, adjusting my pillow.

"You heard what the doctor said. It's too early to tell anything. So we'll just hope and pray that your kidney starts functioning correctly and we can move past everything else."

"It's not that simple, Mom."

"If you would all please leave the room, I would like to talk to Julia in private," she spoke as she shooed everyone out.

\*\*\*\*

# Ellery

I sat down on the edge of the bed and took hold of Julia's hand. Seeing her in so much pain, not only physically but emotionally, killed me.

"I've been where you are, Julia. Different circumstances, but nonetheless, I've been there. You know about my past because we've talked about it before. I know you're scared, believe me. Nobody else will understand the depths of your feelings but me. When I was going through my treatments, not knowing if it would work, I was terrified. Please don't tell your dad this, but even he couldn't erase the doubt in my mind. He had more faith that the treatments would work than I did. You will get through this, baby. You have so much support and so many people to lean on, and that's exactly what I want you to do. If you need a transplant, we'll find a donor. Believe me when I say that your dad will go to the ends of the earth to find one. If you need dialysis, then so be it. You'll make it work. You're a strong woman, Julia Rose, but it's okay to be weak every now and again and I want you to know that I'm here for you when it's just too much to handle."

Tears fell from her eyes and she began to sob. I leaned over and wrapped my arms around her, hugging her lightly.

"It's not fair, Mom."

"I know it's not, baby girl."

"I feel like my whole life just changed in the blink of an eye and I can't handle it. All I keep thinking about is Jake and Brayden. What if something happens to me and they're left all alone? Brayden needs me, Mom, and so does Jake."

"Nothing's going to happen to you because we won't let it. You're alive, Julia, and that's all that matters. We can deal with the rest. It's time to focus on the present and not the future. You need to take things one day at a time and one step at a time."

I wiped the tears from her face and handed her a tissue to blow her nose. "Thanks, Mom. I love you."

## A Forever Family

"I love you too, baby girl."

The door opened and Connor cleared his throat. "Is it okay to come back in now?" he asked.

"Yes, Connor. Tell everyone they can come back in."

I gave Julia a small smile and a wink as I gently squeezed her hand. "One day at a time, baby."

Connor and I stayed with Julia and Jake while Collin took Amelia home and he went to the office. Someone had to be there to oversee things, even if it was only for a couple of hours.

As I went down to the coffee bar to get coffee for me and Connor, I was texting Peyton and not paying attention when I bumped into someone.

"Oh, I'm so sorry," I said as I looked up at the woman staring at me.

My heart started to pound fiercely and a rage crept up inside me as I stood there and stared at the woman I hated most in the world.

"Ellery," Ashlyn spoke with nervousness.

I swallowed hard and it took every ounce of strength in my body not to punch her in the face. I won't lie and say that it wouldn't have given me great pleasure.

"Excuse me," I said as I stepped to the side and began to walk away.

"Ellery, wait. I want to tell you how sorry I am about Julia's accident."

I stopped dead in my tracks and slowly turned around. "How do you know about that?"

"I'm a volunteer and I was here the night they brought her in. I'm sorry. It must be hard for you."

With pursed lips and a closed fist, I stared at the woman who tried to destroy my husband and my family. "My daughter is none of your fucking business. Now I suggest you move along before I attack you like I've done twice before."

"I understand," she spoke as she looked down. "But I'm not that same woman anymore. I've changed. People can change." She walked away and I let out a breath.

I closed my eyes for a moment to compose myself. I ordered two coffees and headed back to Julia's room. Connor was under enough stress as it was and I wasn't about to tell him about my run-in with Ashlyn.

As I was walking back to the room, I saw Mason and Brayden walking down the hallway.

"There's my sweet boy." I smiled.

"Aw, Elle. Thanks, baby. I love you too." Mason grinned.

"Very funny, Mason." I took Brayden from him as he took the coffee cups.

When we stepped inside the room, Julia's face lit up when she saw me holding Brayden. Mason set the coffee cups down and covered his mouth as he stared at Julia.

"My little princess," he began to sob as he raced over to her and gave her a light hug.

*A Forever Family*

Connor looked at me and rolled his eyes. "So much for his spiel about staying strong."

I couldn't help but laugh as I handed Brayden over to Jake.

## Chapter 22
## Collin

A few days had passed and Julia was scheduled to come home from the hospital tomorrow. Mason moved in with Jake to help with Brayden and we all tried to get on with life as normally as possible, with the exception of my mom, who wouldn't leave Julia's side at the hospital.

I shut down my computer, changed into my workout clothes, and told Ethan I was leaving for the day. When I arrived at the gym, Liam was already on the treadmill.

"Hey, bro."

"Hey, Collin. Finally escaped the madness of the office?"

"Yeah. What a day." I smiled.

"How's Julia doing?"

"She's getting out tomorrow. She has an appointment with the nephrologist to go over all her test results."

"I'm praying for her, man."

"Thanks. She really appreciated you stopping by to see her. How did that blind date go the other night that Adam set you up with?"

He looked at me and rolled his eyes. "She was nice and all, but there was no chemistry. She was actually quite boring. I don't know, man. I think I'm just giving up."

"Have you tried a dating site?" I asked.

"Now you sound like Delilah. She's been trying to get me to join one."

"Do it. It won't hurt. Or try that speed dating thing."

"Nah. I'm just going to stop looking. It's not worth it anymore. The problem is that all these women know who I am and a majority of them see dollar signs. I've played the field for far too long. I don't want to play anymore. I want the real thing."

"Hey, why don't you take Sophie to the park? Chicks love men and their daughters."

"She's not my daughter."

"I know that, but they won't know that at first." I chuckled. "Use her as woman bait."

"You need to remember who you're talking about. My niece isn't your average five-year-old. She'd be on to me and then tell Oliver and Delilah."

We got off the treadmill and grabbed some weights. I hated seeing my friend in such a dating funk.

"You'll meet her someday. Just like I met Amelia; by accident and by chance." After lifting a few more weights, we called it a night.

On my way home, I stopped by the hospital to see Julia. Walking into her room, I found myself surprised that she was alone.

"Hey, sis." I gave her a kiss.

"Hey, little brother."

"Where is everyone?"

"Mom and Dad just left with Brayden and Jake went to get some coffee. Hailey stopped by earlier."

"That was nice of her. Was she okay?"

"She seemed to be."

I sat down in the chair next to her bed. "Since it's just you and me, tell me how you're really doing?"

Her lips formed a small smile, but the sadness in her eyes was still there. "I'm scared."

I took hold of her hand. "Listen, if you need a kidney, I'm giving you one of mine."

"Thanks, Collin, but no. I would never ask you to do that."

"You don't have to ask because I'm doing it anyway regardless of what you say. I'm your brother, so I have to be a perfect match, right?"

"I'm not sure. I would think so."

"Then it's settled. It's not fair that I have two kidneys and you have one. That way, if I give you one of mine, then we'll both be known as the Black siblings who only have one kidney."

## A Forever Family

She laughed. "You're a dork."

"I know." I winked. "I have to get home to my wife." I leaned over and kissed her goodbye. "One more night here, sis. Tomorrow, you'll be home where you belong with your husband and baby."

"Bye, little brother. I love you ten times over."

"Bye, sis. I love you more twenty times over." I winked.

****

The next morning, I sat down to a great breakfast that Amelia made before heading to the office.

"You know. I'm getting used to this whole breakfast thing in the morning. It's kind of nice. Maybe you should just stay home and not work."

She glared at me. "Why? So I could cook your breakfast every morning?"

"Yeah. Something like that," I said with a wide grin.

She threw a piece of bacon at me before sipping her coffee. "If you want a homemade breakfast every morning, then maybe you should hire a maid."

I shrugged. "I could, but it wouldn't be as good. You give your breakfasts a sexy little touch."

She rolled her eyes and I chuckled. "I have no response to that, Mr. Black."

I looked at my watch and got up from my chair. "I have to go, babe. I'm interviewing drivers this morning." I bent over and gave her lips a soft kiss. "Damn, you taste good."

"I taste like bacon."

"And I love bacon." I winked as I headed to the door.

I arrived at the office and Ethan followed me in with a cup of coffee.

"Thanks, Ethan. What time is my first interview?"

He glanced at his watch. "In about fifteen minutes."

"Great. Is my dad in yet?"

"Yes, and he's not in a very chipper mood."

I frowned. "Hmm. Okay." I got up from my desk and headed to his office. I lightly knocked on the door, and when I opened it, he was standing with his hands in his pockets, staring out the window.

"Dad?"

"Yes, Collin."

"What's wrong?"

He turned around and I could see the sadness displayed across his face. "Today is the day we get the news about Julia."

I slowly walked over to the front of his desk. "I know. But we have it figured out."

"What do you have figured out?"

"If Julia needs a kidney, I'm giving her one of mine."

"It just doesn't work like that, son."

"I know, but I'm her brother and we're made up of the same genetics, so I have to be a match."

"I'm proud of you, son, and I wouldn't expect anything less from you. We'll just have to wait and see what happens. I'm going to be heading to the hospital soon."

"I should go too, Dad."

"I need you here, Collin. But I will call you when we find out anything."

"Thanks. I have to go. I'm interviewing drivers."

The corners of his mouth slightly curved up. "Good luck with that."

I interviewed six people and none of them measured up to my expectations. Hell, what were my expectations anyway? I was looking for another Denny and when the applicants weren't measuring up, it was way too easy to dismiss them. Was I even being fair? Hell if I knew.

I started to worry about Julia and I was surprised that I hadn't heard anything yet. Just as I was about to call Amelia, my phone rang.

"Hey, Dad. Did you hear anything?"

There was complete silence for a few moments.

"Dad?"

"It's not good news, son. Your sister needs you right now."

"I'm on my way." My heart sank and nervousness settled inside of me.

## Chapter 23
## Julia

Hearing the words, "I'm sorry, Julia, but your kidney is failing," was the hardest thing I ever had to hear. I lay on the couch, clutching my son and never wanting to let him go. Even though I knew deep down that this was going to happen, I wasn't prepared. Could anyone ever be prepared? The doctor told me that I would need to start dialysis right away until they found a donor if I wanted to go ahead with the transplant. Once Collin and Amelia arrived, we had what my dad called a family meeting.

"Since Julia's blood type is O, she can only receive a kidney from another blood type O person. Collin, you aren't type O and neither am I."

"But I am." My mom began to cry. "Unfortunately, because of my two bouts of cancer and the aggressiveness of the last treatment I had, I'm not a candidate."

My dad placed his arm around her and pulled her into him. "I called Cassidy and she's the same blood type as me."

"Jake what about you?" Collin asked.

"I'm type AB." He slowly shook his head.

"Amelia?"

"I'm type A."

"How can nobody in this fucking family be type O except for Mom?" Collin yelled. "This is bullshit, Dad."

The stress that my family was under wasn't helping me and I was ready to explode. Brayden began to fuss, so Mason took him from me. "I don't want a transplant. So I want everyone to stop worrying about me. I've made my decision before I even knew what the final outcome was. I have an appointment with the nephrologist in a couple of days. I've done my research and people who are on dialysis live healthy, normal lives. Now if you'll all excuse me, I'm going to my room. I'm sorry."

I carefully got up from the couch and walked down the hall to my bedroom. I just couldn't take the sadness from everyone anymore. I needed to be alone with my husband and my son.

****

## Ellery

"Julia, wait," Connor said as he tried to follow her.

I grabbed hold of his arm. "Let her go, Connor. I know what she's going through and she needs to be alone for a while. We've been doing nothing but hovering over her since the accident."

I gave Jake and Brayden each a kiss goodbye and went upstairs to the penthouse. Connor, Collin, and Amelia followed. I walked over to the bar and poured myself and Amelia a glass of wine. Feelings that I never wanted to feel again began to haunt me.

"Ellery, how can you just walk out on her like that? She needs us."

"She needs her husband and her son right now, Connor. Julia is a woman; she's not a child and we can't tell her what's best for her. She needs to figure out what's best for her on her own."

"Like you did?" Connor spat.

"Julia's circumstances are different."

"Bullshit, Ellery!"

"Mom. Dad. Please don't," Collin spoke.

"There's only one cure for this and that's a transplant. Do you think I want to sit and watch my daughter go through dialysis for the rest of her life?"

"A transplant isn't a guaranteed cure, Connor!" I yelled back. "The chance of rejection is greater than it taking."

"I'm not discussing this anymore. I'm going upstairs."

I set my glass down on the bar as Connor left the room. Collin walked over to me and pulled me into an embrace.

"I'm sorry, Mom."

"It's okay. Your father is angry and he'll come around. Why don't the two of you go home and get some rest?"

"Are you going to be okay?"

"I'll be fine, Collin." I placed my hand on his cheek.

As soon as they left, I went upstairs and found Connor sitting on the edge of the bed. Seeing him sitting there like that brought back memories of all those years ago. The pained look on his face, the sadness in his eyes, and the hopelessness that resided in him was unbearable to see again. I sat down and placed my arm around him.

"I'm sorry, Elle." He began to cry.

"Don't apologize, baby. I know how bad this hurts, but we'll get through it. Julia will get through it. It's her decision, Connor. Not ours."

"I know, but she's my baby girl, my princess, and I can't just stand by and do nothing." He turned his head and looked at me, bringing his hand up to my face. "I love you and I love our family and I'll do anything to keep all of you safe."

My lips curved into a small smile. "I know, but sometimes there are situations you can't control. We're going to stand by Julia's decision. We'll be there for her every step of the way and we'll support her."

He leaned over and brushed his lips against mine. He needed me physically just as much as I needed him.

\*\*\*\*

## Collin

Climbing into bed, I pulled Amelia into me and kissed the top of her head. I was hurting for my family, especially Julia.

"I think everyone needs to support Julia's decision," Amelia spoke as she ran her hand along my arm.

"I'll be honest with you. I don't know what to think. If Julia can have a better life with a transplant, why the fuck wouldn't she opt for that?"

"It's a hard decision and there's so many factors involved. Don't forget, I took care of patients every day. I know what they go through both physically and emotionally. In Julia's eyes, dialysis is the best option right now."

"My dad won't stop, you know."

"He'll have to. It's not his decision. Maybe one day, Julia will change her mind."

"Maybe." I sighed. "Good night, baby. I love you." I gave her a gentle squeeze.

"Good night, babe. I love you too."

The next morning, I stopped at Starbucks before heading to the office. I didn't get much sleep because my mind was too busy thinking about Julia. I pulled out my phone and called the office.

"Hey, Ethan. It's Collin. I'm running late this morning and I'm in a monstrous line at Starbucks. Can I grab you a coffee?"

"That's so nice of you. If you wouldn't mind, I'll take a grande skinny caramel macchiato with two pumps nut syrup and a dash of cinnamon."

"Do me a favor and text that to me." I chuckled. I shook my head as I ended the call.

"You sure do look exactly like your father." I heard a woman's voice speak from behind.

I turned my head and it was her, the woman I helped on the street. Staring at her for a few moments, the words my father said replayed in my mind.

"I know who you are, Ashlyn, and I would appreciate it if you didn't speak to me, ever. Just go on and pretend you don't even know who I am."

"I'm sure your father has told you all about me, but I can assure you that I'm not that same person I was all those years ago. I have no intention of bothering you or your family."

"Then why are you speaking to me? Just go about your business and pretend you don't know me."

"I really don't know you, but I can tell you're a very nice man. I never properly thanked you for helping me that day on the street. So thank you. I appreciate it. It's rare these days that people would stop and help a stranger."

"You're welcome. Now if you'll excuse me, it's my turn to order."

Grabbing my two cups of coffee, I headed down the street to Black Enterprises. I was faced with the dilemma of whether or not I should tell my dad that I ran into Ashlyn. I decided against it. He didn't need that added stress. He was already dealing with enough and I didn't want to make things worse. But it would only be a matter of time when he ran into her himself and I didn't want to be around when that happened.

## Chapter 24
## Connor

A couple of weeks had passed and Julia started her dialysis. She had asked that we didn't come right away the first day since she was going to be there a few hours and she only wanted Jake there. Ellery and I had taken Brayden for a while until we went to the hospital to relieve Jake. When we walked in, a sick feeling overtook me. The blue reclining chairs lined up against the wall. The machines. The I.V. poles that were placed in each section reminded me all too much of when Ellery was getting chemo. If this was this hard for me, I could only imagine what Ellery thought. I swallowed hard as I saw my princess sitting there, reclined back in the chair hooked up to a machine. Tears began to fill my eyes and I needed to get a hold of myself. I couldn't fall apart on her.

"Hey, princess." I smiled as I kissed her head and handed her Brayden.

"Hi, Daddy. Hi, Mom." Ellery bent down and gave her a kiss, grabbing hold of her hand and holding it tight.

"How are you doing, baby?" I asked with concern.

"I'm doing fine, Dad. Stop worrying about me."

"That's the problem, princess. I'll never stop worrying about you."

She gave me a small smile and sat Brayden on her lap.

Jake, I'm going to get some coffee. Why don't you come with me?" I spoke.

He followed me out of the room and I stopped in the middle of the hall and looked at him. "I know how you're feeling right now and it's okay."

"It's so hard watching her go through this, Connor. I don't know how strong I am."

I placed my hand on his shoulder. "You're a lot stronger than you think. One of the hardest things I ever had to do was watch Ellery go through the most horrific treatments of her life. The pain, the screams, the crying, the doubt. It was so much to handle and, at times, I didn't think I was going to make it through. But then, I would look at her and just think about how much I loved her and my strength pulled us through. Julia needs you to be her strength."

"I know and I promise I will be."

"If you ever just want to talk and let everything out, you know where to find me."

"Thanks." He smiled.

Julia had another hour and a half left and I desperately wanted to be alone with my daughter. Brayden was crying on and off and he looked so tired.

"Jake, take him home and put him down for a nap," Julia spoke.

"I don't want to leave you, baby."

I looked at Ellery. "Since Julia only has about an hour and a half left, why don't you go with Jake and help with Brayden. I'll bring Julia home when she's finished."

She knew exactly why I wanted her to leave and she was more than happy to oblige.

"Come on, Jake. Let's get this little guy settled and get things ready around the apartment for when Connor brings Julia home."

Jake leaned over, gave Julia a kiss goodbye, and then left with Ellery. I took hold of my daughter's hand.

"How are you doing?"

"I'm doing fine, Daddy. Please don't worry about me."

"Did I ever tell you about the time that I went to your mother's first chemo treatment?"

"No." She grinned. "But somehow, I think it's a hell of a story."

"Your mom and I weren't seeing each other anymore and I had sent Denny to follow her to see where she went, what she did, but most importantly, that she was okay."

"So you had Denny stalk Mom?"

"Yes. I did, and I'm not ashamed to admit it."

Julia laughed as she interlaced our fingers. "Go on. I'm dying to hear the rest of it."

"I found out that she decided to do the chemo treatments and I showed up at the hospital, this same hospital, in fact, and she was not happy to see me. She was such a smart ass. I can remember it like it was yesterday. Her attitude sucked and she gave me so much grief. She tried to kick me out numerous times, but I wasn't going anywhere and she wasn't telling me otherwise. When her first treatment was over, I took her home and made her pack because I didn't want her staying in that box of an apartment by herself. She told me that she wasn't my charity case and to know that she felt that way really hurt me. But ultimately, she packed a bag and stayed briefly at the penthouse. One day, I was in my office and I heard her whimpering upstairs. When I went up to check on her, I found her lying in the hallway, curled up in a ball and crying. She was in so much pain that she wouldn't let me touch her. I felt so helpless. Finally, she told me to pick her up and get it over with. When I did, she screamed and cried. That is one day I'll never forget. A few days later, I said some things I shouldn't have out of anger and she left and went to California without as so much as a word."

Julia slowly shook her head at me. "Wow. You two are so stubborn. I would give anything to be able to travel back in time and watch the two of you."

"It wasn't easy, but I never once gave up on her. Just like I'm never giving up on you, princess."

"I know this is hard for you, Dad, considering what you went through with Mom all those years ago. But please don't worry; I'll be okay. I promise. I'm strong and I can do this. We'll have to make some minor adjustments, but life will go on."

A single tear fell from my eye as I stared into the eyes of my little girl. "Life will go on, princess."

"Dad, there's something I need to tell you." She reached over and wiped away my tear.

"What is it, baby?"

She looked down and, suddenly, I became worried.

"That night of the accident when they took me to surgery, something happened."

She paused.

"Julia, what happened?"

"I had a dream, but I don't think it was a dream. I saw Denny."

I narrowed my eyes at her and cocked my head. "What do you mean you saw Denny?"

"One minute I was in the operating room on the table, and the next I was standing in the hallway outside the room. He told me that it wasn't my time and that I had my whole life ahead of me."

I swallowed hard as another tear filled my eye. "Did he say anything else?"

"He told me to tell you to stop being stubborn and that you know the right thing to do and that forgiveness always prevails. He said that everything happens for a reason and the big guy upstairs makes things that way. He looked so good, Dad, and he said he was happy and had never felt better."

I knew at that moment that Julia was telling the truth. Denny had written in his letter that forgiveness always prevails and nobody knew that but me and Ellery. I squeezed her hand as I bent my head down and rested it on her. Knowing that Denny was happy and at peace gave me comfort.

"Dad, are you okay?"

I lifted my head. "I'm fine, princess. Thank you for telling me. Why didn't you tell me sooner?"

"I don't know. So much had happened. Do you think I'm crazy?"

"No, Julia." I smiled. "You're not crazy at all."

"Do you know what Denny meant about forgiveness and you being stubborn?" she asked.

"No. Not really." I let out a light laugh.

Her dialysis was finally over and I helped her out of the chair and into the limo where Ralph drove us to our building.

****

Later that night, after Julia got home and settled, Ellery and I went back to the penthouse and placed a carryout order. Grabbing the plates from the cupboard, she set the table and I opened the wine. A few moments later, the doorbell rang and our Chinese food had arrived.

"Julia told me something today that is really sticking with me."

"What did she tell you?"

"She said that she saw Denny the night of the accident when she was in surgery."

"Oh?" She smiled. "What did he have to say?"

I sighed. "He told her to tell me to stop being stubborn and that I know what the right thing to do is. He also said that forgiveness always prevails."

She set down her chopsticks and her eyes widened as she stared at me.

"Yeah. I was just as shocked as you are right now."

"I don't know what to say, Connor. Denny did say in his letter that he'd always be watching over us. I guess he is and, to be honest, it's very comforting to know that he was there for Julia."

"Yeah. The man is dead and yet he's still telling me what to do." I smiled.

Ellery laughed and we finished our dinner, took a nice hot bath together, and then made love to each other into the late hours of the night.

## Chapter 25
## Collin

Stroking her soft beautiful breast, I wrapped my lips around her hardened nipple. The soft moan that escaped her lips turned me on even more. My fingers traveled down her torso and stopped the minute I felt her swollen clit. When I traced around it with small circles, her hips thrust into me, begging me for more. I loved to tease her, but what I loved most of all was making her come. My fingers found their way inside, feeling her pleasure and the warmth that emerged from her. My tongue traveled around her breasts, all the way down to her hips and finally stopping at her sweet aching spot that was begging for a release. The flicker of my tongue against her clit drove her insane.

"Collin, please. Deeper, faster, baby."

"Patience, my wife. It's all about control." My tongue swirled around her, licking and sucking her lips until she was about ready to lose control. "Let me enjoy you first before I fuck you into oblivion." I looked up at her and smiled as I took hold of her legs.

"If you don't make me come now, I will finish myself off and kick you out of this room, leaving you with the worst blue balls you've ever had!" she said in an authoritative tone.

Hearing her say that got me so damn turned on that I flipped her over so she was on her stomach and I thrust inside her as hard as I could. I was like an animal, thrusting in and out of her at a rapid speed.

"Is this what you want?" I groaned as I grabbed hold of her ass as hard as I could.

"Yes. Oh yes, baby. That's it. Make me come all over your hard cock."

Jesus, I wasn't ready to come yet, but she had me so fucking turned on, I couldn't hold back anymore. Three more pumps inside her and she screamed my name as I did hers and we both came together. My heart was rapidly beating and my skin was wet from sweat. I spilled every ounce of myself inside of her before collapsing on top of her, trying to catch my breath.

"Fuck, Amelia. You had me so turned on I couldn't stop myself."

She giggled and reached around, tangling her fingers in my hair. "Excellent way to start my first day of work."

I climbed off of her and gave her a kiss. "We better get ready. You don't want to be late for your first day and I have a meeting to get to."

We showered, got dressed, and parted ways for the day. "Have a good first day and I'll see you later, baby."

When I arrived at the office, Ethan told me that Julia wanted to see me. It was her first day back. Smiling, I walked into her office and took note of the numerous flower arrangements that were scattered all around.

"Welcome back, sis!"

*A Forever Family*

"Thank you for the flowers, little brother, but one arrangement would have sufficed."

"So Ethan got a little carried away. I think it looks and smells great in here." I kissed her cheek and then took a seat across from her desk. "You looked tired. Are you sure you're ready to be back here?"

"I am very tired and, yes, I'm ready to be back."

"You're only here part time. Don't forget that and push yourself."

"I won't. With my dialysis schedule, it's going to be hard to work full time anyway. I have to go four times a week and it sucks."

"Have you considered maybe just staying home and taking care of yourself and Brayden?"

"I can't. I'd go crazy. I love working here and when Dad retires, he's going to need both of us."

"Just take it easy, sis."

My phone rang and I pulled it from my pocket, noting a call from Max Hamilton.

"I have to take this. I'll talk to you later. Hey, Max. What's up, buddy?"

"Can you meet me, Oliver, and Liam for lunch today? I have a proposal for you about a new piece of software my company developed."

"Sure. Where and what time?"

"The Four Seasons Restaurant on East 52$^{nd}$ Street at one o'clock."

"Sounds good, bro. I'll be there."

"Great. See you then."

I went to my dad's office and once again found him staring out the window.

"Do you ever do any work?" I chuckled.

"It doesn't seem like it these days. Thank goodness I've trained you well." He smiled as he took a seat in his chair. "What's up?"

"I'm meeting Max for lunch. He wants to pitch some new software his company developed."

He slowly nodded as he leaned back. "Good. You decide if it's worth it. I'm leaving the decision to you."

"Thanks, Dad. By the way, Amelia and I talked about it and we want to postpone the wedding reception. With everything going on with Julia, we just don't think it's the right time."

His eyebrow arched. "Have you told your mother this?"

"Not yet. I wanted to run it by you first."

"I will personally castrate you, little brother, if you even think about postponing that reception."

I turned around and Julia was standing in the doorway. I swallowed hard. She walked in and handed Dad a file.

"Sorry, Julia. We just want to wait."

"Bullshit, Collin. You're having that wedding reception as planned. When are you people going to learn that life will go on as normal?"

I put my hands up. "Fine. Okay. We'll still have the wedding reception."

"Good. Now if you'll excuse me, I have a dialysis appointment to get to."

"Do you want me to go with you, princess?"

"Thanks, Dad, but Mom is meeting me there with Brayden."

"Good luck." He winked at her.

\*\*\*\*

I stepped inside The Four Seasons restaurant and the hostess showed me to Max's table where I shook everyone's hands before taking my seat.

"How's Julia doing?" Liam asked.

"She's putting on a brave front, but I think deep down, she's falling apart."

"Sorry, bro," Max spoke.

I sat and listened as Max pitched his new software. He had a great concept and he executed it flawlessly. After discussing business, we talked about personal matters.

"Are you all coming to my wedding reception next month?" I asked with a grin.

"Wouldn't miss it for the world." Oliver smiled.

"Kara and Molly are taking Sarah for the weekend so Emma and I can stay in the Hamptons."

"That's great, Max. You two deserve some time alone. Are you bringing a plus one, Liam?"

"I don't know yet. We'll see. If not, I'll just tag along with Oliver and Delilah."

I happened to look across the restaurant and I saw Hailey and Marcus getting up from a table. It looked like they were arguing. As Hailey was about to walk away, I saw Marcus grab her arm and pull her back and not in a nice way. He had anger splayed all over his face. She tried to get out of his grip, but he wasn't letting go.

"Excuse me for a moment, gentleman." I got up from my seat and walked over to where they were standing.

"Hailey. Marcus. Fancy seeing you here. How are you?"

"Hi, Collin."

"Hey, man. We're great. How are you?"

"I'm good. Thanks, Marcus. Just having a business lunch."

Hailey wouldn't look at me. She kept her head down and her eyes focused on the floor.

"Is everything okay, Hailey?"

"Of course. Why wouldn't it be?" Marcus asked. "Go back to your business lunch, Collin. Hailey and I have some things we need to do. Have a good day."

He took Hailey's hand and led her out of the restaurant. She turned her head and looked at me for a brief moment and all I saw were her apologetic eyes. I walked back to the table and took a seat.

"Everything okay with Hailey?" Liam asked.

"I don't think so," I said as I stared at the restaurant door.

## Chapter 26
## Julia

The fatigue was getting worse. The muscle cramps, especially in my legs, were getting worse. There were some days that I could barely walk, no matter how hard I pushed myself. This was becoming unbearable. I was doing everything right. I was eating properly, taking fifteen different vitamins a day, and drinking more water than I ever had in my lifetime. Nothing was helping me and my doctor said I would have to learn to deal with it because they were the side effects of dialysis. I tried to be strong, but I could feel myself sinking into a deep depression. My sex drive was gone and I didn't have the energy to make love to my husband anymore. Jake was supportive and said he understood. But it had been weeks since we'd had sex and it wasn't fair to him. Fuck, it wasn't fair to me. I cried every day and asked God why. I was tired of the sympathetic looks I got from people at the office when I would limp down the hallway. I put on a fake smile every day in public, but behind closed doors, I was nothing but a train wreck. Jake knew it and my family knew it.

"Are you ready to go, babe?" Jake asked as he grabbed our suitcase from the bed.

"Yeah." I yawned.

## A Forever Family

We were driving with my parents to the Hamptons. Tomorrow was Collin's wedding reception and I just wanted to get through it. I put Brayden in his car seat and my dad carried him downstairs for me.

"Do you want to sit in the front, Julia?" my mom asked.

"No, Mom. I'll be fine in the back with Brayden and Jake."

Jake held my hand the whole way to the Hamptons and Brayden was a good boy and slept. When we pulled into the driveway, I got out of the car and went to grab my suitcase.

"I got it, princess. You just go inside," my dad spoke.

It seemed lately that I was being treated as if I couldn't take care of myself and I didn't like it. I went inside the house and my mom followed.

"Is there anything I can do to help for the party tomorrow?"

"No, sweetheart. We really don't have to do anything. The maids were already here to clean and the decorators and caterers will take care of everything tomorrow morning."

"How many people are coming?" I asked.

"About three hundred."

"Jesus, Mom. You should have had it at the Waldorf."

"Your brother wanted it here. We have plenty of room, so don't worry."

"I'm not worried. Why do you think I'm worried about it? It just seems like it would have been easier to have three hundred people at the Waldorf than here. But it's your party, so whatever." I needed some air, so I took a walk down to the beach.

****

# Connor

I looked at Julia as she flung open the door and walked away from Ellery.

"What the hell was all that about?"

"I'm not sure. I'm worried about her, Connor."

I wrapped my arms around her and pulled her into me. "I'll go talk to her."

Just as I was getting ready to walk out, Jake walked in the kitchen with Brayden. "Where's Julia?"

"She went down to the beach and she just snapped at Ellery."

Jake sighed as he handed Brayden over to Ellery. "She's been on edge lately. I try to talk to her, but she insists everything is fine."

"I'm going to talk to her now."

I walked down to the beach and saw Julia sitting down in the sand near the shoreline.

"Hey, princess. What was all that about back there with your mom?"

"Nothing, Dad. I'll apologize to her. Don't worry."

Sitting down and bringing my knees to my chest, I wrapped my arms around them and looked at my daughter. "Tell your old man what's really going on."

## A Forever Family

"I don't know, Daddy. I just feel like everyone is treating me like I'm disabled or something. People are babying me. It's as if they think I'm going to break."

"Nobody thinks that."

"Yes they do. You even do it too."

The truth was, I did baby her. I couldn't help it. "I'm sorry, Julia."

"As soon as we get back to the city, I'm calling Dr. Benson. I want to go ahead with the transplant and I want to be put on the list. Dialysis is too much for me. I thought it would be a piece of cake, but it's not. I spend half my time and days sitting in that damn chair. Not to mention the side effects. I just can't do it anymore, Dad. I feel like I'm missing my son's life." She wiped the tears that fell from her eyes.

"We have to find a match, princess."

"Dad, I love you, but please, just let me be put on the list. I don't want you investing time in me like that. You have other things to worry about."

I put my arm around her and she laid her head on my shoulder. "You're my daughter and I will invest my entire life in you. There is nothing that I wouldn't do for you."

"I know, but please let me do it my way. Please, Dad. I'm begging you."

I sighed as I kissed the top of her head. "Okay, baby, if that's what you truly want."

There was no way I was going to sit back and let her be put on some list that could take years for her to even get a call. I would explore all options without her knowing. I would stop at nothing to make sure my daughter got what she needed.

We got up from the sand and dusted ourselves off before walking back up to the house. As soon as Julia walked in the kitchen, she gave Ellery a hug and apologized to her.

"Can you two watch Brayden for me? I need to talk to Jake alone."

"Of course we will. You two take as much time as you need." I smiled.

She and Jake left the house. Ellery set Brayden on the floor and gave him his toys.

"Did you have a nice talk?"

"Yes. We did. Our daughter has decided she wants to go ahead with the transplant. She's going to call the doctor first thing Monday morning to get on the list."

Ellery glared at me. "You're going to do something about that, right?"

The corners of my mouth revealed a small smile. "Of course I am. I'm surprised you would even ask."

She walked over to me and wrapped her arms around my waist. "Just making sure."

## Chapter 27
## Collin

Amelia was in the kitchen and I was upstairs changing into my wetsuit to go surfing. There was a knock at the door and I was sure it was Julia, so I yelled to Amelia that I would answer it. I flew down the stairs and when I opened the door, standing there were Diana and Jacob.

"Oh my God!" I hugged Diana tightly and then Jacob. "I thought you two couldn't make it?"

"Yeah. I lied." Diana gave me a bright smile.

"We wanted to surprise you," Jacob said in excitement.

"And you did. God, it's so great to see you. Come in."

They stepped inside and Amelia came into the foyer and gave them both a hug. She looked at me and smiled.

"You knew they were coming. Didn't you?"

"Maybe." She gave me her cocky grin.

I couldn't stop staring at Jacob and how tall he'd gotten since the last time I had seen him.

"Wow. You, my man, are growing up so fast." I placed my hand on his head. "You up for some surfing?"

"Yeah!" He smiled.

"Great. Let's go! Diana, come down to the beach with us."

"Diana and I will be down there in a while." Amelia leaned over and gave me a kiss.

Jacob and I grabbed the surfboards from the garage and headed down to the beach. "Have you been feeling okay?" I asked as I put my board in the water.

"Yeah. I've been feeling really good. I met a girl."

"Is that so? I want details. Is she hot?"

"Yep, and she's a great surfer too. I really like her."

We paddled away from the shore. "What's her name?"

"Brooklyn."

"Do you have a picture?"

"Yeah. I have several on my phone. I'll show you when we get back to the house."

I held up my hand and we high-fived. It was so good to see him again and be able to spend time with him. I was really bummed when Diana said that they wouldn't be able to make it when I last talked to her, but now, I was so happy they were both here.

We surfed for about an hour and headed back to the house to change and get ready to go to my mom and dad's for dinner. I jumped in the shower, and when I got out, Amelia was brushing

*A Forever Family*

her hair. She turned to me as I wrapped a towel around my waist. Placing her hands on my chest, she reached up and brushed her lips softly against mine.

"Are you happy?"

"Very happy." I smiled.

"Good. Now you have exactly twenty minutes to get ready because your mom moved up dinner." She laughed.

I rolled my eyes and sighed. "Why does she always do that shit?"

Amelia patted me on the chest and walked out of the room. I changed into some clothes, dried my hair, and made it down to my parents' beach house with two minutes to spare. Diana and Jacob were already there, chatting it up with my family.

\*\*\*\*

The reception was just starting and everyone was settling into place for dinner. Amelia and I were getting ready to make our grand entrance and the event coordinator spoke into the microphone.

"Attention. May I have your attention? I would like to welcome everyone here tonight on this beautiful evening to celebrate and congratulate Amelia and Collin. If you're ready, please direct your attention to left and welcome Mr. and Mrs. Collin Black."

Everyone began to clap and whistle as Amelia and I made our entrance holding hands and smiling. I took Amelia up to the stage where the band was set up and I took the microphone from the planner's hand.

"I want to thank all of you for coming tonight and celebrating with us. This woman right here. This beautiful, God-given gift is the love of my life and I couldn't wait to marry her and make a lifelong commitment with her. She's what every man dreams of and she's all mine. I love her and she loves me and we didn't want to wait, so we got married in Vegas."

Clapping, whistling, and the clanking of glasses filled the air as I turned to Amelia and we kissed. "I want everyone to have fun tonight! So let's get this party started!" I yelled in excitement.

We stepped off the stage and headed to our table for dinner. White tents filled the patio and large open area before it met the beach with round tables covered in white linens, white floral arrangements, and beautifully lit candles, which sat in the center of each table. White lights were strung throughout the tents, giving the atmosphere pure romance. After we ate an incredible meal, Amelia and I made our rounds and talked to our guests.

"Hey, Peyton. Henry. Where's Hailey?"

"She called and said she wasn't feeling well. She thinks she has the flu," Henry spoke.

I knew it probably would have been hard for her to be here, so I didn't really blame her. Amelia went to talk to some of her college friends and I went over to see what kind of conversation was going on between my assistant, Ethan, and Liam.

"You aren't trying to steal my assistant out from under me, are you, bro?" I smiled.

"Maybe I am." He winked at Ethan.

Ethan patted me on the back and walked away. We continued the evening with drinks, laughter, and dancing.

## A Forever Family

Delilah took the stage and sang a few of her songs for us and everyone seemed to be having a great time. It was exactly what Amelia and I had envisioned. I walked over to where my mom was and gave her a big hug.

"Thanks, Mom. This is amazing. Amelia and I are so grateful to you and Dad for doing this for us. I love you."

"Aw, my sweet boy. You're welcome. But I'm still mad you got married without your family being there."

"I know, but can you please not stay mad too long. I hate when you're mad at me." I kissed her cheek.

"You're forgiven." She smiled. "I love you and Amelia very much."

The party went into the wee hours of the morning and Amelia and I headed home to do some celebrating of our own. I insisted that Diana and Jacob stay at our house, but she said that they were staying with my mom and dad because newlyweds should be left alone. Amelia and I were going to meet them for breakfast in the morning because they were flying back to California in the afternoon so Diana could get back to work at the gallery.

## Chapter 28
## Julia

My head was pounding and I felt so weak that I couldn't even get out of bed to get Brayden when he woke up in the morning. Jake tended to him and, when he came back, he was surprised I wasn't getting ready for work.

"Julia, are you okay?"

I shook as I pulled the covers up to my chin. "I don't think so."

He placed his hand on my forehead and then ran to the bathroom to get the thermometer.

"Baby, you're burning up." He slid the thermometer in my mouth.

When it beeped, he read it and looked at me. "I'm calling your mom to watch Brayden. You have a 104 fever and I'm taking you to the hospital."

"No, Jake. I just want to stay in bed. Please. No hospital."

"It's not up for discussion, Julia. Something is obviously wrong." He walked out of the room and I rolled over, pulling the covers up over my head.

Within moments, my mom and dad entered my room.

"Julia, get up, sweetie. You need to get dressed." My mom pulled the covers from me.

"Princess, this is no time to play around."

Now I was aggravated. "I'm not playing around, parents. I don't want to go to the hospital. Just give me some ibuprofen and the fever will go down."

"Sorry, but with your kidney problems and that fever, you're going to the hospital."

Jake walked in with Brayden. "I just got off the phone with the doctor and he said you are to get to the hospital immediately. He's already there, tending to another patient, so he'll be in to see you as soon as he can."

I sighed as I tried to sit up but couldn't. I was so weak that I couldn't even see straight.

"Connor, go. I'll help Julia get dressed and then we need to get her into the limo. Make sure Ralph is downstairs."

My mom went into my closet and pulled out one of my sundresses. "This will be the easiest to get on, Julia," she said as she lifted my night shirt over my head and tossed it to the side. She slid the sundress over me and I couldn't help but lie back down. She got up from the bed and went to get Jake and my dad.

"Jake, go downstairs and put the car seat from your car into the limo and strap Brayden in. I'll bring Julia down. Come on, princess; let's go."

My dad lifted me from the bed. I placed my arms around his neck and laid my head on his chest as he carried me to the limo. He carefully slid me inside and I laid my head down on Jake's lap while my mom sat with us and Brayden and my dad climbed in the front with Ralph.

We arrived at the hospital and the nurses were waiting for me. They immediately brought a wheel chair to the limo, lifted me out, and wheeled me to a room in the ER. An IV was immediately placed in my arm and the nurse wasted no time drawing all kinds of blood. Jake and my parents were in the room with me as I closed my eyes. All I wanted to do was sleep.

****

# Collin

I was sitting in my office, working up some numbers for a huge meeting with Daniel Durant and his associates, when my dad walked in with Brayden. I looked up and instantly could tell something was wrong.

"Dad, why do you have Brayden?"

"Listen, son. We had to rush your sister to the hospital this morning and I need you to keep an eye on Brayden for us."

I got up from my chair and took him from his arms. "What happened? Is she okay?" I asked with worry.

"She has a 104 fever and she's very weak. Jake, your mom, and I are staying at the hospital with her and you're the first person I thought of to look after Brayden. I guess I could have called Peyton, but I wasn't thinking clearly."

"It's okay, Dad. He'll be fine here with me. Tell Julia I'll be by after work. Will you keep me informed about her condition?"

"I will, Collin. I have to get back to the hospital. I'll talk to you later."

As soon as he left, Brayden started to fuss. "Oh no, little man. Don't be sad. Your mom is going to be okay." I didn't know who I was trying to convince, me or him. I was worried sick about Julia and I felt helpless. The office door opened and Ethan stepped in.

"Is everything okay?" he asked.

"They had to take Julia to the hospital. She's really sick."

"Oh no. She'll be okay, Collin. Don't worry. Is there anything I can do?"

"Can you go get the playpen and toys from Julia's office and bring it here?"

"Sure thing, boss."

I took Brayden over to look out the window. "See this view, buddy? This will be your view someday. You're going to grow up and work for your mommy and your uncle and this could be your office one day."

He cooed and I smiled as I kissed his head. A few moments later, Ethan came in with the playpen and toys and set it up for me. I set Brayden down and scattered his toys all around him with the hopes that he'd stay occupied for a while. I had to get these numbers finished and into the proposal for my one o'clock meeting.

I looked up at the clock and it read 12:55. I closed the file, grabbed it, took Brayden from his playpen, and stepped out of my office. I looked around and Ethan was nowhere to be found and neither was Laurinda. *Shit*. I needed them to look after Brayden while I was in the meeting with Durant. I stood there for a few moments, and neither one of them showed up.

"Well, it looks like you're attending your first business meeting, little man. Make sure to take notes on how it's done." His eyes were focused on my file as he tried to reach for it.

I walked into the conference room and Durant and his associates were already seated.

"Mr. Black," they spoke with their French accents as they stood and we shook hands.

"Thank you, gentlemen, for agreeing to this meeting." I took a seat and set Brayden on my lap. He started to cry. *Shit*. I smiled at the men and got back up, walking around the table. He stopped crying. I guess he didn't want to sit down.

"Mr. Black, we weren't aware that you had a child," Durant spoke.

"He's not mine. He's my nephew. My sister had to be rushed to the hospital this morning. She's very ill."

"We are sorry to hear that."

"Thank you, but let's get on with this meeting, shall we?"

I conducted the meeting by walking around the room, holding Brayden. The minute I even attempted to sit down, he would start to cry. If Durant hadn't flown in from Paris for his meeting, I would have rescheduled.

"Your nephew is very cute, Mr. Black. Would you mind if I held him?" one of the associates asked.

"Uh, sure." I handed Brayden over to him.

I continued on with my proposal and none of them were paying attention. They were all too busy fussing over Brayden. Durant looked at me.

"Mr. Black, you seem like a great man and we've heard many wonderful things about your father and this company. Not many businessmen would conduct an important meeting like this with a baby in his arms. You took care of your nephew and conducted this meeting like a true professional."

"Why, thank you, Mr. Durant."

"I can tell you're a good family man and we would be happy to do business with Black Enterprises." He smiled. "We take family values very seriously at Durant Inc."

My heart began to race. This wasn't a decision to make lightly. I didn't expect an answer from Durant for at least a few months. This was incredible.

"Thank you, Mr. Durant." I smiled as I walked over and shook his hand. "You won't be sorry about your decision."

"I'm sure I won't be." He took the pen from the table and signed the agreement.

"Now, we better get going. We want to explore the city before we leave for Paris. My wife would love this little guy." He took hold of Brayden's hand and Brayden cooed at him.

His associate gave Brayden a kiss and handed him back to me. "Have fun in New York and I'll be in touch."

They walked out of the conference room and I started doing a little dance with Brayden. "Thank you, little man. How does it feel to have landed your first deal?"

## Chapter 29
### Connor

Julia was in and out of sleep most of the day. Finally, around three o'clock, the doctor walked into the room. It infuriated me that we'd been here since this morning and we still had no answers.

"I have the results of your bloodwork and it seems you have a bacterial infection. I've had the nurse start you on a round of strong antibiotics and you should be feeling better in a few days. Until then, you'll need to stay in the hospital and get plenty of fluids and rest. And I'm sorry to tell you this Julia, but no contact with your son. Not until the infection has cleared up."

"But, Dr.—"

"No buts. This is very serious," he spoke.

Julia's eyes filled with tears as Jake squeezed her hand. "It'll be okay, baby. It's only for a few days," he spoke.

"I've also gone ahead and put you on the transplant list."

"How long?" I asked.

He sighed. "It can be weeks, months, or even years. Because of her age, she's down on the bottom of the list. There are others who are in more desperate need of a kidney than Julia."

"That's bullshit!" I snapped and Ellery placed her hand on my arm.

"I know it's frustrating, Mr. Black, and I would feel the same way if it were my daughter. My advice to you is to see if you yourself can find a match. But I will tell you that not a lot of people are just willing to give away their kidney. I'll be by in the morning to check up on you, Julia. Until then, get some rest."

I rubbed the back of my neck as I walked over and stared out the window. Suddenly, Julia screamed.

"I HATE THIS! IT ISN'T FAIR!"

I turned around and Ellery and Jake were by her side, trying to calm her down as she cried. The pain on her face and the sadness in her eyes was too much to bear. I stepped out of the room and called Collin.

"Hey, Dad. How's Julia?"

"She has a bacterial infection. Can you and Amelia keep Brayden until your mom and I come home? Julia can't see him for a few days until the infection clears up."

"Shit. Yeah, of course we can. I want to come by and see Julia. Amelia will be off work soon, so I'll drop Brayden off at home and then swing by. There's something I need to tell you."

"Good news, I hope."

"Great news. I'll see you soon, Dad."

I hung up and walked back into the room. Julia had seemed to calm down. I walked over to her and pressed my lips against her forehead.

"Collin and Amelia are going to keep an eye on Brayden until we get home. He'll be stopping by later."

She nodded her head and closed her eyes. Ellery and I stepped out of the room and went down to grab some coffee. Before we made it to the coffee bar, Ellery suddenly grabbed my arm and led me down an isolated hallway. Pushing me up against the wall, she smashed her mouth into mine. I didn't know what the hell had gotten into her at that moment, but I wasn't complaining.

****

# Ellery

As Connor and I were on our way to the coffee bar, I saw Ashlyn standing there talking to someone. She didn't see us, but I couldn't let Connor see her. I grabbed his arm and led him down a hallway, pushed him up against the wall, and passionately kissed him. He was going to question me about what I had just done, so I had to come up with something quick.

"Baby, what the hell was that for?"

"Are you complaining?"

"Of course not, but we're in a hospital."

"So what. It never stopped *you* before. I just felt like I needed to do that. We both needed it, Connor."

He placed his hand on my cheek and softly brushed his lips against mine. "You're right. We did need it, didn't we?"

I gave him a small smile as I pulled him from the wall and hugged him, staring out and making sure Ashlyn was nowhere in sight.

"Okay. I really need that coffee now."

He chuckled. "Let's go and get it, then."

I was a nervous wreck. It was only going to be a matter of time before he saw her and then, when he did, the shit was going to hit the fan full force.

****

## Connor

Shortly after we got back to Julia's room, Collin walked in. He went over to her, kissed her head, and asked her how she was doing. Ellery, Jake, and I took a seat over on the small couch by the window so the two of them could talk. If anyone could talk to her, it was him. After their conversation, and Julia smiled, Collin walked over to us.

"What's this great news you have to tell?"

"Let me guess!" Ellery shrieked. "Amelia's pregnant!"

"Good God. No, Mom. I closed the Durant deal, Dad."

"What?" I looked at him in confusion.

"I had that meeting with Durant today."

"No, son. That meeting was for tomorrow."

"No, Dad. It was today. Anyway, I had to take Brayden in the meeting with me because our secretaries were at lunch. Durant and his associates loved Brayden and they loved how I was with him and how I put my family first, so they signed the deal."

"Right there on the spot?"

"Yep."

I was speechless at that moment. That deal had just made our company millions of dollars and my son closed it at the proposal. Even I had never done that. I reached over and gave him a hug.

"Good job, Collin. I'm so proud of you."

"Thanks, Dad."

Even though Collin was more than ready to take over Black Enterprises, Ellery and I had talked, and considering Julia's accident, handing over the company to them in three months was put on hold until we knew for sure how long this would affect Julia's life.

## Chapter 30
## Collin

The next day, after I visited Julia in the hospital, Liam and I went out for dinner and a drink. Amelia was going out with her girlfriends to celebrate one of their birthdays, so I used the opportunity to hang with Liam and have some guy time. We ended up at a bar for some burgers and beer. As we were talking, eating, and having a good time, my phone rang. I pulled it from my pocket. Hailey was calling.

"Hello," I answered.

"Collin. I need your help. Please." She sounded like she was crying and her voice was really low.

"What's wrong, Hailey?"

"I need your help."

"Where are you?"

"516 West 71st Street. Apartment 6B."

"I'll be there soon." I ended the call and asked Liam to come with me.

When we arrived at the building, we took the elevator up to Hailey's apartment. I didn't even know she lived here. I knocked on the door and there was no answer, so I placed my hand on the knob, and it opened.

"Hailey?"

I saw her sitting on the couch with her knees up to her chest. As I walked closer, I noticed the glass coffee table was filled with drug paraphernalia. She looked up at me with blood dripping from her nose and her eye was swollen.

"Did Marcus do this to you?" I asked calmly as I sat down next to her.

She nodded her head and then began to cry. Liam went into the bathroom, grabbed a washcloth and handed it to me.

"What happened, Hailey?" I gently wiped the blood from her nose.

"We got into a huge fight."

"Where is he now?" I asked in anger.

"I don't know." She continued to cry. "He took off. I'm so scared of him. I thought he was going to kill me."

I pulled her into me to comfort her. "You can't stay here."

"I can't tell my mom and dad. Please, Collin."

I sighed. I didn't know if I was doing the right thing or not. I looked up at Liam as he slowly shook his head.

"You're staying with me and Amelia tonight and I'm calling the police."

Her head shot up and a look of terror swept over her face. "No police. He'll kill me, Collin."

I placed my hands firmly on her shoulders, gripping them tightly. "Listen to me, Hailey. This ends tonight. I know he's been hurting you and I know you're hooked on drugs. If you want my help, you're going to do exactly as I say. We're going to my place. I'm calling the police, and you're going to press charges against him. Tomorrow morning, you're going to call your parents and then you're checking yourself into a treatment center to get help. You called me because you want me to help you. So this is me helping you."

"I'm scared."

I pulled her into me. "There's nothing to be scared of. You have a lot of people who love you and are going to support you. You need to get your life back on track, Hailey. If you don't, I can't help you."

She nodded her head and I helped her up from the couch. "Go pack a bag and let's get out of here before he comes back."

She walked to the bedroom and I turned and looked at Liam.

"What's Amelia going to say about this?" he asked.

"I don't know. I guess I'll find out right now." I pulled my phone from my pocket and dialed her.

"Hey, baby," she answered. "I just got home. I'm surprised you aren't home yet."

"I need to talk to you about something."

"God, what happened, Collin? I can hear it in your voice."

"I'm bringing Hailey home with me and she's going to stay in the guest room tonight. She's in bad shape and I need you to look at her."

"What happened?"

"She and Marcus got into a fight and he beat her."

"Oh my God. When will you be here?"

"About twenty minutes. I'll explain the rest later."

"Okay. I love you."

"I love you too and thank you."

I ended the call and placed my phone back in my pocket.

"Boy, you better thank your lucky stars Amelia is such a wonderful and caring woman. I don't know too many women who would be willing to take in their husband's ex-girlfriend."

I gave him a small smile. "She's the most incredible woman in the world."

Hailey came out with her bag and I took it from her. We climbed in Liam's car and he drove us back to the bar so I could get my Range Rover. I helped Hailey in and then gave Liam a light hug.

"Thanks, bro, for everything."

"No problem, man. Call me and let me know how she's doing."

When we arrived home, Amelia came from the direction of the kitchen and stopped when she saw Hailey.

"Come here," she said as she walked over and wrapped her arm around her shoulder and led her to the couch. "I'm going to get some ice for your eye."

"I'll get it, baby. Just sit with her."

I went into the kitchen and wrapped some ice in a towel and handed it to Amelia. She gently placed it over Hailey's eye and she flinched.

"It's okay, Hailey. Just relax. When and what type of drug did you last use?"

Hailey looked at her and then at me. I could tell she didn't want to answer her.

"It's important you tell me."

"I did some coke about two hours ago," she replied.

"Okay. Hold this over your eye. I'll be right back. Collin, follow me, please."

I followed her into the kitchen as she placed her hands on the counter. "She's going to start going through withdrawal in about five hours, maybe sooner. What are you planning to do with her?" she asked.

"First thing tomorrow, I'm calling the police, and then she's checking into a rehab center."

"You need to tell her parents."

"She's going to tomorrow. Right now, she just needs to sleep this night off." I wrapped my arms around my wife and hugged her tight. "Thank you for this."

"No problem. She needs help really bad and I think you're the only person that can convince her to get it."

\*\*\*\*

Amelia and I didn't get much sleep. A thousand things were going through my mind and I couldn't shut my brain down. Not only was I dealing with Julia's situation, I was now dealing with Hailey's.

I climbed out of bed around six a.m. and went into the kitchen to make a pot of coffee. Amelia wasn't too far behind as she joined me in the kitchen. Around seven a.m., Hailey walked in and Amelia poured her a cup of coffee.

"How are you feeling?" she asked her.

"Like I've been hit by a train." She took the coffee cup and sat down at the table. "Listen, I'm so sorry to involve both of you in this. I didn't know who else to call."

I sat down next to her and placed my hand on hers. "I'm glad you did call. You need help, Hailey, and you can't deny that. He could have killed you."

"I know." Tears sprang to her eyes.

"I'm going to call the police now and then you need to call your parents. They have to know what happened."

"I can't, Collin. Can you call them for me? I'll fall apart and I'm not feeling real good right now." She was shaking.

"Fine. I'll call Peyton and tell her what happened."

I walked out of the kitchen and to my bedroom. Picking my phone up from the nightstand, I dialed Peyton.

"Good morning, Mr. Black," Peyton answered.

"Good morning, Peyton."

"I'm a little worried that you're calling me so early. What happened?"

"Can you and Henry come by my place as soon as possible? Hailey's here and she needs you."

"What the fuck happened to her?"

"She and Marcus got into a fight and he hit her."

"WHAT?!" she yelled. "We're on our way." *Click.*

I dialed the police and told them what happened. They were sending out two police officers right away.

Before long, there was a knock at the door, and when I opened it, Peyton and Henry stormed in.

"Where is she?" Henry asked calmly.

"In the living room."

They walked in and the minute Hailey saw them, she broke down and sobbed along with Peyton. It was heartbreaking to watch as Amelia and I stepped out of the room to give them some privacy. A few moments later, two police officers showed up and took Hailey's statement.

My phone rang and I grabbed it from the kitchen counter to see that my dad was calling.

"Hey, Dad."

"Hi, son. Your mom and I are going to visit Julia in about an hour. Do you and Amelia want to ride with us?"

"Sorry, Dad. We can't right now. We sort of have a situation."

"What situation?"

I explained to him what happened and before I knew it, he and my mom came racing into the apartment. The police officers left and Peyton helped Hailey into the shower. Henry walked over to me and placed his hand on my shoulder.

"Thank you, Collin, for helping my little girl last night. Considering your history together, that was very nice of you to still want to help her."

I gave him a small smile. "You just can't throw away years of history because things didn't work out. Where is she going?"

"We're taking her to the Odyssey House. A friend of mine is the director there and I just called him. He's getting her room ready as we speak."

Hailey and Peyton walked back into the room and it was time to say goodbye. She looked at me and the sadness in her eyes made my heart ache. I walked over to her and took both of her hands in mine.

"You can do this, Hailey. You're better than the drugs. It's time to get your life back."

"I know. Thank you again for not turning your back on me."

"I'll come visit you," I said as I hugged her.

"You better because, right now, you're the only friend I have."

"That's not true," Amelia spoke as she walked over to her. "I'm your friend too and you have our full support. You can call us at any time." Amelia hugged her.

"Thanks, Amelia. Are you ready, Mom? Dad?" She took in a deep breath.

Peyton patted my shoulder as they walked out the door. Once it closed, my mom walked over and hugged me.

"Thank you, my sweet boy. You're an amazing man."

"I know I am, Mom. I have the genes of two amazing parents." I smiled as I kissed her head.

## Chapter 31
## Connor

It was three days since Julia had been hospitalized and, depending on her bloodwork, she was scheduled to go home tomorrow. Jake's parents took Brayden for a few days so Jake could spend his time with Julia. I called every family member I knew and no one was too keen on getting tested to see if they were a match for Julia. I was furious and I let my mother know it as she was in the room visiting Julia with us. While we were all talking, the doctor walked in with a smile on his face.

"I have good news for you, Julia. We found you a donor."

"What?!" she asked in excitement. "How so fast?"

Happiness overtook me when I heard the doctor speak those words but also an uneasiness washed over me because it had happened so quickly.

"Someone came forward with the same blood type as you and asked to be tested. Once all the tests were completed, she turned out to be a viable donor and she's agreed to donate one of her kidneys to you."

"Who is she?" Julia asked.

"I can arrange a meeting with her if you'd like."

"Yes. Please. I want to thank her for helping me."

"Okay, Julia. I'll arrange it. Depending on your bloodwork tomorrow, you will probably be able to go home and, once you meet your donor, I can go ahead and schedule the operation within the next couple of weeks."

"Thank you. I can't believe it."

"There still are some kind people in this world." He smiled as he walked out of the room.

Ellery had tears running down her face as she hugged Julia. This was the best news we'd gotten in a long time and it finally seemed like things were coming together. We left the hospital so Jake and Julia could celebrate in private and met Collin and Amelia at Per Se for dinner. He was overjoyed with the news, but he had the same concern I did. Ellery and Amelia excused themselves to the restroom, which gave me and my son a chance to talk in private.

"Who do you think is helping Julia?" he asked.

"I don't know, son. I'm a little concerned myself."

"I'm happy for her, Dad. Don't get me wrong, but I'm a little on the fence."

"I am too. Maybe we're overthinking this and she's just a very nice woman who wants to help your sister. I have to believe that there are some helpful, loving people left in the world."

"Yeah. Maybe you're right."

## A Forever Family

Ellery and Amelia came back and took their seats, and we enjoyed a nice dinner celebrating the good news.

****

The next morning, Ellery and I dropped by the hospital to see Julia on my way to the office. I was in an exceptionally good mood. Between the amazing sex Ellery and I had last night and a good night's sleep, nothing could ruin the way I felt. I couldn't wait to see Julia and kept my fingers crossed that she was being released today. I lightly knocked on her hospital door before entering.

"Come in," she said. "Daddy, I would like you to meet the woman who's giving me her kidney."

I stopped in the doorway when the woman turned around. My legs felt as heavy as lead and they would not allow me to take another step. My heart started to race and it felt like it was getting harder to breathe.

"Hello, Connor," she spoke as she looked down.

"What the fuck do you think you're doing, Ashlyn?" I said in a stern voice.

"Ashlyn?" Julia said with confusion in her voice.

"Get the fuck out of my daughter's room NOW!" I yelled.

I lunged towards her and Ellery grabbed my arm. "Connor, stop. Not here."

This was nothing but a nightmare and I needed someone to pinch me to wake me up. Anger rose inside of me and it was only the hold Ellery had on my arm that was stopping me from choking that bitch to death.

"What's going on?" Julia pleaded.

"Connor, let me explain. Please," Ashlyn begged. "I want to help your daughter."

My breathing became rapid as I stood there, unable to see anything but the woman that nearly destroyed my life and my family.

"You aren't going to say anything. You are to get the fuck out of here before I have you thrown out!" I yelled.

Ashlyn put her hands up in defense. "Ellery, please calm him down. Let me explain."

"Connor. Please, calm down for Julia's sake. This is a hospital that is full of very sick people."

I turned around so I didn't have to look at Ashlyn to try and collect myself. The rage that was inside scared me. I could have very easily killed her right then and gone to jail and I wouldn't have given a damn.

"You have one minute to explain yourself," Ellery said to her.

"I am a match for your daughter, who needs a kidney, and I'm willing to give her one of mine as an apology for all these years. I want to help you and your family, Connor. I want to make amends."

I whipped myself around and Ellery grabbed my arm again. I jerked out of her grip and pointed my finger directly in Ashlyn's face. "Make amends? You're incapable of making amends. You're nothing but a cold-hearted, psychotic bitch who deserved everything she got. You should still fucking be in prison as far as I'm concerned, and there's no way in hell

I'm letting them put your kidney in my daughter's body. You are my sworn enemy and nothing you can do or say will ever make things right."

"I'm not that woman anymore. I've had years of therapy and I've changed. I'm married to a wonderful man and we're very happy. I don't want to harm you or your family. I only want to make things right."

I paced around the room, rubbing the back of my head, trying to calm down. But with each word she spoke, the angrier I became. There was no forgiveness here. There never could be.

"Your husband obviously doesn't know the real you."

"Yes, he does. He knows all about my past and he accepted me."

"Then he's more fucked up than you are!" I scowled.

"Daddy! Stop!" Julia began to cry. "This is my decision. This is my life, not yours. Now get out of here!"

"Princess." I looked at her as tears filled my eyes.

"Daddy, I love you, but I can't sit here and listen to you. I don't even know who you are right now and, to be honest, I don't like you like this."

My heart broke as I saw the disappointment splayed across her face. I sat down in the chair and cupped my face in my hands.

"Forgiveness always prevails, Daddy."

I looked up at my daughter and stared into her eyes. Denny. Denny's words. Ellery didn't say anything. She just stared at me with sadness in her eyes.

"I can't do this." I got up from the chair and stormed out of the room. I heard Ellery call my name, but I didn't stop; I just kept going. I took the stairwell down to the first floor, and when I reached the doors, I hailed a cab and had the driver drop me off in the parking garage at my apartment building. I climbed in the Range Rover and drove to the beach house.

## Chapter 32
## Connor

I arrived at the beach house and, when I walked inside, it felt strange to be in the house by myself. I walked over to the bar and poured a scotch and took it outside on the patio. My phone kept ringing. When I looked at it, I saw that I had four missed calls from Ellery and three missed calls from Collin. Obviously, she told him what was going on. As soon as I set my phone down, a text message from Collin came through.

*"Dad, you're freaking us all out. Where are you?"*

I did the unthinkable and turned my phone off and hid from my family. I just wanted to be left alone. Ashlyn, the memories, and the hell that bitch put me and my family through all those years ago was something I'd never forget. I never wanted that woman back in our lives, and now to find out that she, the one person I hated the most in this world and wanted dead, could save my daughter's life was too much to fucking handle.

I went inside and grabbed the bottle of scotch and took it down to the beach. As I sat in the sand and stared across the ocean, I started to talk to Denny.

"If there was ever a time I needed you, old man, now is it. How the fuck am I supposed to accept something like this? You told me in your letter and to Julia that forgiveness always prevails. Maybe it does. But not in this case; not where Ashlyn is concerned. How do I look at my daughter every day, knowing that she has an organ in her that once belonged to the one person I despised the most on the face of this earth?" I brought the bottle up to my lips and tilted my head back, taking more than a small drink. "How the hell do you forgive someone who nearly destroyed you? Who nearly cost you the woman of your dreams and the love of your life? The same person who threatened my daughter when she was just a baby?" I took another drink as tears streamed down my face. "Damn you, Denny. Damn you for dying and leaving me here to face this on my own!" I took another drink and, before I knew it, the bottle was almost empty. "At least tell me something. Don't just leave me here like this, old man."

It was at that moment when I swore I felt someone place their hand on my shoulder. I quickly turned around, but no one was there. I took the last sip of scotch and fell over in the sand.

****

# Ellery

"Are you sure he's there, Mom?" Collin asked me as we drove to the beach house.

"If there was one place he'd go to, it's there."

Watching Connor's reaction to Ashlyn reminded me of the day Kyle told him I had cancer. The look on his face, the hate in his eyes, and the tone of his voice was something I had never wanted to see again. And for the first time, since that day, I saw that side of my husband. I didn't blame him, though. How could I? I sighed. Collin reached over and took hold of my hand.

"Don't worry, Mom. We'll find him and, hopefully, he's calmed down. Do you really believe that Ashlyn's changed?"

"I don't know what to believe. All I know is I need to get to your father."

"We'll be there soon, Mom. Try to relax."

I could see the Range Rover parked in the driveway from down the street. I let out a sigh of relief as Collin pulled up. I flew out of the car and into the house, calling Connor's name. He didn't answer. I saw that the liquor cabinet over the bar was open and I told Collin to go upstairs and see if Connor was in the bedroom.

"No, Mom. He's not up here."

I began to panic as I walked outside to the back. I saw the glass sitting on the table and, when I looked down to the beach, I saw Connor lying in the sand.

"He's out here," I yelled to Collin.

I knelt down beside Connor and noticed the empty bottle of scotch. Collin came running down and stood beside him.

"Yep. I know what that's like."

I shot him a look and told him to help me get Connor up to the beach house.

"Come on, Connor. You're drunk and you need to get to bed."

Collin and I pulled him up.

"I want to be alone," he slurred.

"Well, that's just too damn bad. Running away from situations was my thing, Mr. Black. Not yours. And when you're sober, we're going to have a discussion about you turning off your phone."

"I love you, Elle, but you need to be quiet."

A cocky smirk crossed Collin's face as he looked at me.

"You think this is funny, young man?" I said in a stern voice.

"No, Mom. Not funny at all." He laughed.

We got Connor into the house and up the stairs. After laying him on the bed, Collin and I went downstairs.

"He'll be out for a few hours and, when he wakes up, I don't know what he's going to do."

"I'm sorry this is happening, Mom," Collin said as he wrapped his arms around me. "Dad just needs some time to process all of this. We all do. Why don't we order a pizza and we can sit down and try to figure things out."

"Go ahead and order the pizza but as for trying to figure things out, it's not up to us to figure anything out. Like Julia said, it's her decision and her life and there's nothing we can do to stop it."

****

## Connor

I opened my eyes and looked around the room, wondering how I had gotten in bed. I glanced over at the clock and it read ten p.m. When I climbed out and unsteadily walked downstairs, I saw Ellery and Collin sitting on the couch.

"Ellery," I spoke.

She got up and walked over to where I was standing, wrapped her arms around me, and laid her head on my chest.

"You had me so worried, Connor."

"I know and I'm sorry. I just needed to get out of there." I held her head tightly against my chest.

"Hey, Dad," Collin said as he placed his hand on my shoulder.

"Hey, son."

"Now that I see you're okay, I'm going to head back to the city."

"It's late. Stay the night and head back in the morning," I spoke.

"The night is still young, and besides, you two need time alone to talk. Plus, I want to get home to my wife." He walked away and before he reached the door, he stopped. "By the way, you told Mom to be quiet." He snickered. "Good luck, Dad."

*Shit*. "Thanks, Collin."

"You better be careful driving home!" Ellery yelled as he walked out the door.

"Did I really tell you to be quiet?" I asked with a hint of fear in my voice.

"Yes, you did."

"Can you yell at me tomorrow? I really want to go back to bed."

"Of course I can wait. But be prepared to get an earful in the morning." She smiled.

I sighed and wrapped my arm around her as we walked up the stairs and went to bed. I didn't want to talk about Ashlyn and Ellery knew it. That was why she never brought it up. We climbed in bed and she wrapped her body around me as I held her tight.

The next morning, I felt soft lips pressing against mine. I opened my eyes to see my beautiful wife staring at me.

"Good morning." I smiled.

"Good morning. We need to get up, talk, and then head back to the city."

I sighed. "Are we talking or yelling?"

Her mouth curved into a small smile as she ran her fingers across my forehead. "No yelling. I've decided to let yesterday slide. But we do need to discuss Julia."

She climbed out of bed and slipped on her robe.

"Ellery," I called out.

"Yes, Connor?" She turned her head and looked at me.

"No cocktail today. I'm fine."

"Okay. I'll go start the coffee." She winked.

I got out of bed, took a shower, and got dressed. When I walked into the kitchen, Ellery handed me a cup of coffee. We went outside and sat down on some beach chairs she had set up down by the water.

"I'm not okay with all this, Elle. I will admit to you that I'm scared. That woman is up to something. People don't just change like that."

"I know what you mean, Connor, and I don't like it any more than you do. In fact, I hate it. It makes me sick to my stomach seeing her and knowing that Julia would trust her enough to let her donate her kidney to her. But it's Julia's decision and she has hope. Hope that only a stranger can give her." Tears started to fill my eyes. "We have to trust our daughter. We have no other choice. I think that we need to talk to Ashlyn in a calm and rational manner and really get a feel for her sincerity."

"I can't talk to that bitch, Ellery. You know that. Just looking at her turns me into a different person. A person that I don't like."

She reached over and took hold of my hand. "I know, but we have to do it for our daughter, for our son in-law, and especially for our grandson. Jake needs his wife and Brayden needs his mother."

What Ellery spoke was the truth and it made me sick to my stomach to think that I would have to try and hold a civilized conversation with Ashlyn.

## Chapter 33
## Connor

As Ellery and I drove back to the city, her phone rang. It was Julia calling. She had been released from the hospital and was home. Instead of going straight to the penthouse with Ellery, I knocked on Julia's door. Jake answered.

"Hey, Connor." He gave me a light hug.

"Where is she?"

"She's in the bedroom changing. She'll be out in a minute. I'm going to go up to the penthouse to leave you two alone so you can talk."

"Does she even want to speak to me?"

"I'm sure she does. She's still really upset."

He patted my shoulder and walked out the door. Julia came out from the bedroom and stopped when she saw me standing there.

"Hi, princess." I smiled.

"Hi, Dad. Where's Jake?"

"He went up to the penthouse so we can talk."

"Then let's talk." She sat down on the couch and I sat next to her.

"I'm sorry for everything, princess. I just wish she wasn't the one."

"I know that, but she is and she's willing to help me. After you stormed out of the hospital, we talked for a long time. She told me what a horrible person she was back then and how sorry she was for what she did to you and Mom. I do believe that there's some good in her. This is her way of trying to repent for all her mistakes. This is my chance, Daddy. My chance at regaining my life back and if it's her kidney that will give me that, then so be it. You can't protect me forever. I'm an adult, a wife and a mother, and I make my own life decisions."

Tears sprang to my eyes when she reached over and placed her hand on mine.

"I want to protect you from all things bad, Julia. I made a promise to you when you were a baby that I would always be here for you. To guide you and to protect you from the evils of this world."

"And so far, you have. But there are some things you can't control and me accepting Ashlyn's kidney is one of those things."

"I know, princess, and I'm sorry."

She reached over and wrapped her arms around me. "I love you, Dad."

"I love you too, baby."

\*\*\*\*

I had Laurinda do some digging around and get me Ashlyn's phone number. I leaned back in my chair as a sickness washed over me when I dialed her number.

"Hello," she answered.

"Ashlyn, it's Connor. We need to talk."

"Okay, but only if you promise not to behave like you did the other day at the hospital."

"You have my word." I clenched my fist as I felt the burning anger flow throughout my body.

\*\*\*\*

As Ralph pulled up to Ashlyn's home, I closed my eyes and took in a deep breath. This was probably the hardest thing I ever had to do—facing the enemy who was the only person at this moment who could save my daughter. We walked up the steps to the brown brick home and Ellery squeezed my hand as she rang the doorbell. The door opened and a man, Ashlyn's husband, I presumed, stood there staring at us.

"Hello, you must Connor and Ellery. I'm Thomas, Ashlyn's husband." He held out his hand to me.

I shook his hand, and as we stepped inside the foyer, Ashlyn walked down the stairs. I could tell she was nervous.

"Hello, Connor. Ellery." She nodded.

I took in a sharp breath because I wasn't so sure anymore if I could do this. My palms were sweating and all I could think about was getting this over with as we followed them into the living room.

*A Forever Family*

"I know how hard this must be for the both of you," Thomas spoke. "I know all about Ashlyn's past and the things she did to you. Please believe me when I tell you that she isn't that woman anymore."

"That's to be determined," I said in a harsh voice.

"Please sit down. Can I get you a scotch, Connor?" Ashlyn asked.

"No. I just want to get this over with so we can be on our way. Why don't you start by telling me why you're doing this and what your agenda is?"

She sat down in the dark green wing-backed chair across from me and Ellery. "I don't have an agenda, Connor. I'm doing this because your daughter needs help and I can help her. Like I told you before, I'm not that same person I was all those years ago. I want to make up for all the mistakes I made back then and live life the best I can." She looked down as she interlaced her fingers together on her lap. "I know I don't deserve your forgiveness and I'm not asking for it. I still can't forgive myself for what I've done, but I can try to come to terms with it. I'm a volunteer at the hospital. I read to the elderly and hold the hands of those who are dying that never get any visitors. I spend a lot of my time volunteering at the food bank and I do work for a lot of different charities. I was in the ER that night they brought in Julia and I was there when they rushed her up to surgery. Believe it or not, I was scared for you and Ellery because I knew if something happened to her, it would destroy the both of you."

I sat there, staring at her, trying to get a grip on her tone, her words, her body language. She was never a hard one to read because she had always been a cold-hearted, manipulative bitch. There was only one time I saw her like this and that was before Amanda committed suicide and she had her heart broken by her boyfriend. It was a night that I stayed with her and talked into the early hours of the morning. Telling her that he wasn't worth it and that she deserved better than him. It wasn't until after Amanda's death that Ashlyn changed.

"It doesn't matter anymore whether you believe my intentions are good, because to me, I know that I'm doing the right thing by Julia," Ashlyn spoke. "I found out years ago that I can never have children. Your grandson needs his mother."

"This is a big thing to do," Ellery said as she looked at her. "And you're okay with this, Thomas?"

"I support whatever decisions my wife makes. If she wants to help your daughter by giving her a kidney so she can live a full, normal life, then I commend her for that."

I sat there and slowly shook my head. This was a losing battle and the decision was already made. It was now up to me to come to terms with it. I got up from the couch and took Ellery's hand.

"We need to get going. Thank you for talking with us and—" I inhaled deeply. "Thank you for what you're doing for my daughter."

"You're welcome."

"It was nice to meet you, Thomas," Ellery spoke as she held out her hand.

"It was nice to meet both of you as well. Thank you for coming over."

I gave them both a small smile and exhaled as soon as we walked out the door.

## Chapter 34
## Julia

My surgery was scheduled for next week but until then, I still had to undergo dialysis. I spent more time being exhausted, but I knew that soon, it would be over. Tonight was family dinner and my mom had invited my grandmother over. When we stepped off the elevator and walked into the kitchen, my grandmother gave me a hug.

"There's my darling granddaughter. How are you feeling?"

"Very tired, Grandma."

She placed her hands on each side of my face. "Soon you'll be feeling like a million bucks again." She smiled.

"Don't I get a hug, Grandma?" Collin said as he held out his arms.

"Of course you do, darling. How are you?"

"I'm good, Grams."

After giving our grandmother a hug, Collin hooked his arm around me and kissed my cheek.

"How was dialysis today?"

"Boring as usual."

"Soon it'll all be over with. You'll have a new kidney and life can get back to normal."

"Hopefully, my body doesn't reject it," I spoke.

He leaned over and whispered in my ear, "It won't because it's Ashlyn's. Your body will accept it just to piss Dad off."

I smacked him on the chest and laughed.

"What are you two whispering about?" my dad asked as he entered the kitchen.

"Just a little private joke between a brother and sister, Dad." Collin smiled.

My mom put dinner on the table and, as we were all eating, my phone rang. I picked it up and noticed it was Dr. Benson calling.

"Hello," I answered.

"Julia, it's Dr. Benson. Are you home by any chance? I'm leaving the hospital now and I'll be passing by your building. There's something I need to talk to you about."

"I'm at my parents' house, which is the top floor penthouse. You can come here."

"I'll see you in about fifteen minutes or so."

"Okay, Dr. Benson."

My stomach instantly felt sick. Why would he have to talk to me?

"Julia, what did Dr. Benson want?" my dad asked.

"He said he needs to talk to me about something so he's coming here."

Jake grabbed my hand. "I'm sure he just wants to go over some things, baby. Don't worry."

"It sounded important. If he just had to go over some things, then he would have scheduled an appointment for me to come into his office."

"Don't get yourself all worked up, Julia," my grandmother spoke. "I'm sure it's nothing."

I was glad my family was feeling so positive about it because I wasn't. Something was wrong and I could sense it in Dr. Benson's voice. I couldn't eat anymore, so I took Brayden from his high chair and went into the living room. About twenty minutes had passed and there was a knock on the door. Collin answered it and led Dr. Benson to the living room. My whole family gathered around.

"Julia, we can speak in private if you'd like."

"No. It's fine, Dr. Benson. My family can stay."

He sighed. "I'm not quite sure how to tell you this, but Ashlyn is no longer a viable donor."

The bottom of my stomach fell out as Jake put his arm around me. I couldn't muster up any words. I was literally frozen.

"Why?" my father asked.

"I'm not allowed to go into detail because of patient privacy, but she can no longer donate her kidney to you. I'm so sorry, Julia. I know how bad you want this. You're still on the list, though, so as soon as I hear something, I'll call you. Until then, you'll have to resume dialysis on a normal basis like you have been."

Tears fell from my face as my hope of getting better was gone, crushed by the mere words of Dr. Benson.

"Thank you, Dr. Benson," my dad spoke as he walked him to the door.

"Oh, Julia." My mom walked over and embraced me. "I'm so sorry."

My dad walked back in and looked at me. "Princess, I'm—"

"Sorry? Is that what you were going to say? Because I don't believe you! You're happy that this isn't happening. You never wanted me to have Ashlyn's kidney in the first place! So don't sit there and pretend that you're sad, Daddy, because you aren't!" I yelled.

I got up from the couch and grabbed Brayden from Amelia's arms. "Jake, let's go." I stormed out of the penthouse and went home.

\*\*\*\*

## Connor

I couldn't believe this was happening as I stood there in the middle of the room while my daughter stormed out.

"She didn't mean it, Dad," Collin spoke. "She's upset. I mean, come on, this is total bullshit. She's crushed."

"I don't understand." I shook my head as I walked over to the bar and poured myself a drink. "FUCK!" I yelled as I slammed my glass down on the bar. "Regardless of how I felt in the beginning, Julia was getting the transplant and she was happy. Now it's been ripped away from her, from us. The chances of her getting that transplant soon are gone. We're back to fucking square one!" I yelled.

My mother got up from the chair and walked over to me. Placing her hand on my shoulder, she spoke, "There's one more person you can try, Connor."

"Mom." I looked at her in anger.

She put her hand up. "It's for your daughter. Your anger is with your father, not Lucas. He didn't ask to be born into this family and he certainly did nothing wrong." She said goodnight and walked out the door. Ellery and I went up to bed.

I looked over at Ellery. She was sound asleep. Me, I couldn't sleep. I had too much on my mind and my daughter was at the forefront. I was devastated for her that the transplant wasn't happening. I climbed out of bed and paced the penthouse. Giving serious thought to what my mother said had me conflicted. But I knew what I needed to do for Julia. There was no price too great for her wellbeing. I climbed back into bed and wrapped my arms around my wife. She reached back and placed her hand on my face.

"I love you."

"I love you too, baby."

## Chapter 35
## Connor

I sat down on the bench in the conservatory gardens and dialed Lou.

"Lou, I need you to do something for me."

"Anything, Connor."

"I need you to find a man named Lucas Oaks, son of Charlotte Oaks. Last known address was Cherry Hill, New Jersey."

"I'll get on it right away."

"Thanks, Lou. I'll talk to you later. Someone just arrived that I need to talk to."

I ended the call as Ashlyn stood in front of me. "Have a seat, Ashlyn."

"I'm sorry, Connor."

"What's going on? Did you change your mind? Was this your plan all along? Get my daughter's hopes up and then destroy them with a snap of your fingers? Was this your revenge, Ashlyn?"

She clenched her jaw as she stared at me, listening to every word I spoke. Her nostrils flared and tears sprang to her eyes.

"I have cancer; lymphoma, to be exact. The lab called because they thought they made an error and wanted me to come in for another blood test. I'm sorry about Julia and if I still could give her one of my kidneys, I would. But you go ahead and still think the worst of me. If you want so badly to believe that I planned this whole thing, then go ahead." She got up from the bench and began to walk away. She stopped and turned to me. "I guess this is my punishment for my past." A tear fell from her eye.

I reached out and grabbed her hand. "Ashlyn, I'm so sorry. I don't know what to say."

"You've said enough, Connor."

"Wait. Please." I got up from the bench and stood in front of her. "You asked me to believe that you'd changed. Now I'm asking you to believe that I'm truly sorry."

She looked away as she wiped the tears from her eyes. "I believe you and thank you. I also understand why it's so hard for you to forgive me. Goodbye, Connor. I hope everything works out for Julia. Tell her I'm sorry and that I have my own battle to fight now."

I nodded. "I will. You can beat this, Ashlyn."

She gave me a small smile as she turned away and walked out of the conservatory gardens. I stood there with my hands in my pockets, preparing myself for my next battle. A battle that involved a man who was my brother. A brother that I'd never met.

\*\*\*\*

I was walking down the hall of Black Enterprises on the way to my office and I heard Collin yelling from his. I looked over at Ethan, who shrugged. As I opened the door, Collin threw his phone across the desk.

"What's going on, son?"

"Hey, Dad. Just people not doing what they're supposed to be doing. I'm having some renovations done on the beach house and the contractor is a dick. In about two seconds, I'm firing his ass."

I laughed as I sat down in the chair across from him. "I've been there myself many times. In fact, I remember almost firing the contractor for our beach house because it almost wasn't done before the wedding. But everything worked out and they finished it. Where's Julia? I stopped by her office and she wasn't there and neither was her secretary."

"She went home because she's so exhausted that she fell asleep at her desk."

"I spoke with Ashlyn earlier."

"Oh? Why?"

"To find out why she was no longer a donor candidate for Julia."

"And?" he asked as he leaned back in his chair.

"She has cancer."

"Oh. That's not good news."

"No. It isn't." I got up from my seat. "I have some work to do and then I'm leaving for the day. I need to go talk to Julia."

"Okay, Dad. Good luck."

I walked out the door and into my office. Just as I sat down, my phone rang and it was Lou.

"Lou, what's up?"

"I have the information you requested."

"Excellent. Let's meet for dinner at six o'clock at Daniel. I'll have Laurinda make the reservation."

"Sounds good, Connor. I'll see you then."

When I looked at the clock, it was already four. I shut down my computer and grabbed my briefcase.

"Laurinda, I'm leaving for the day. I'll see you tomorrow."

"Enjoy your dinner, Connor. See you tomorrow."

When I knocked on Julia's door, I could hear Brayden crying. When she opened it, she was holding him, and when he saw me, he smiled.

"What's wrong with my grandson?" I asked as I took him from her.

"He's teething."

"Ah, I remember going through that with you. Did you give him some medicine?"

"Yes, and hopefully, it will help him soon. I'm so tired, Dad, and Jake won't be home for another couple of hours. All I want to do is take a nap."

I sat down on the couch with him and held him up by his hands. "Did you call your mother?"

"No. I don't want to bother her. She's taken care of him so much already." She curled up on the couch next to me.

"You need to hire a nanny, princess."

"I don't trust anyone with him, Dad. Only family. I wish Mason was here."

A small smile crossed my lips. "Me too."

"So why did you stop by?" she asked.

"I met with Ashlyn today. She has cancer, princess."

"Oh no, Dad. That's terrible. I hope she's going to be okay."

"Me too, Julia."

"Really, Dad? Do you really mean that?" she asked as she cocked her head.

"Yeah. I do. Nobody should have to go through that."

She sighed. "Well, we're back to square one, so I'll just have to deal with it until there's a donor. There isn't anything else I can do."

"Keep positive, princess, and have faith." I reached over and grabbed her hand, bringing it up to my lips. Now go get Brayden's diaper bag. I'm going to take him upstairs with me so you can take a nap. I do have a dinner meeting with Lou at six, but your mom will be home and she'll be very upset if she knew you didn't want to call her."

"Are you sure, Dad?"

"I'm positive. Now go."

Julia got up and went into the nursery. "Grandpa is going to do everything he can to help your mommy. This is what the men in this family do. We stop at nothing until we get what we want."

Brayden smiled and cooed as if he understood me. I kissed his cheek and got up from the couch as Julia handed me the diaper bag.

"Thank you, Daddy. I love you."

"I love you too, princess. Get some rest."

As soon as I stepped off the elevator, Ellery came walking into the foyer. "I thought I heard a baby and a hot, sexy man." She smiled as she kissed me.

"Hi, baby."

"Why do you have Brayden?"

"I stopped by Julia's and told her to take a nap. She looked tired."

"Next question. Why did you stop by Julia's? I thought you were still at the office." She took Brayden from me.

"I met with Ashlyn today. She has cancer, Elle."

She looked at me with wide eyes. "That's awful. What kind?"

"Lymphoma," I said as I followed her to the living room.

"That explains why she's no longer a viable donor."

"Yep. Anyway, I'm meeting Lou at Daniel at six o'clock for a business dinner. We have some contracts to go over."

"Oh, okay. Peyton is coming over, so we'll just order Chinese or something."

I gave her a kiss as I headed up the stairs. "I'm going to change. Maybe you can try to lay Brayden down and join me in the bedroom?" I winked.

She arched her brow. "So you want to ignore our grandchild so we can have sex?"

I stopped on the middle step and looked at her. "We did it with our own kids. Why are grandkids any different?"

She shook her head as she smiled and followed me upstairs. "You're a very bad grandpa, Mr. Black."

"Not bad. Just horny."

\*\*\*\*

"What do you have for me, Lou?" I said as I sat down in the booth across from him.

He slid a file folder across the table. "This one was a little tough. Lucas Black is twenty-eight years old and lives in Vegas. He's an executive chef at Sage and studied at Le Cordon Bleu in Paris for six years before moving back to the States."

I narrowed my eyes as I opened the file. "Wait a minute. Black?"

"Yep. Charlotte gave him your father's last name and listed him on the birth certificate."

"Why would my father agree to that?"

"I don't know, Connor. Maybe he wasn't given a choice. Look further on down in the file. Check out his blood type."

My eyes veered down the paper. "He's type O," I spoke as I looked at Lou.

"Yep. He sure is. What are you going to do now?"

"Looks like I'm going to Vegas to meet my brother and pay him a great deal of money for his kidney."

"Be careful, Connor. I'm sure this boy isn't going to be welcoming you with open arms."

I closed the file and set it down. Taking a drink of my scotch, I knew I needed to devise the perfect plan to get Lucas to listen to me.

## Chapter 36
## Collin

Peyton had told me that Hailey was allowed to have visitors now at the Odyssey House since her detox was over. I thought that maybe it would be a good idea to go visit her and see how she was doing. I grabbed my phone from the desk and called Amelia.

"Hi, babe," she answered cheerfully.

"Hi, good looking. Are you wearing something sexy right now?"

She giggled. "My sexy as fuck blue scrubs. I know how much they turn you on."

She thought she was being funny, but in reality, seeing her in scrubs did turn me on. I liked when she played nurse with me.

"Okay, stop talking like that. I'm getting hard."

She laughed. "You asked."

"Listen, I think I'm going to visit Hailey over at Odyssey. Do you want to come with me?"

*A Forever Family*

"No. I think it's best that you go alone. I'm sure she has a lot to talk to you about. Give her my best, though."

"I will, baby, and when I get home, you better still be in those scrubs. I think I'm coming down with something and I'll need you to check me over, Nurse Amelia."

"Fine. I'll make sure I have all the tools necessary to fully examine you."

"Fuck, Amelia. I better go or I'm going to have a bad situation over here."

She laughed. "Goodbye, Mr. Black. I love you."

"Goodbye, Mrs. Black. I love you more."

I had Ethan call the Odyssey House. Visiting hours started in fifteen minutes. I hopped in the Range Rover and drove there, hoping that Hailey wouldn't be mad at me for stopping by.

I stood in the lobby and waited for Hailey to come down. I was looking around when I heard her voice.

"Hey, Collin."

I turned around and smiled when I saw her. For the first time in a long time, she looked good.

"Hey, Hailey. How are you?"

"I'm okay. Let's go out to the courtyard."

I followed her through the lobby and out the sliding doors that led to a beautiful courtyard made up of different types of flowers, small wrought-iron tables that sat four people, and a few wooden benches.

"Your mom said that you're allowed to have visitors now. That's good."

She looked down at her hands. "Yeah."

I really didn't think this would be awkward, but it was. "You look good, Hailey."

"Thanks. Collin, I'm sorry for everything."

"Nah. Don't be. Shit happens. You did the right thing. Have you heard anything about Marcus?"

"He got deported back to France and he's not allowed back in the U.S. They found a shitload of coke on him when they arrested him. He's France's problem now."

"That's good. At least you won't have to worry about him anymore. What's going on with you, Hailey? Why the drugs?"

"It was only supposed to be a one-time thing. Then one time turned into two and two turned into three. Marcus didn't always hit me. That just started a few months ago."

"Why didn't you break up with him?"

"Because no Marcus meant no more drugs. I've let everyone in my life who loves me down. I let myself down. Marcus stripped me of everything I ever believed about myself. He took away my self-esteem and my dignity. I'm not this person."

Sadness consumed her. Not only in her face but also in her words. I reached over and placed my hand on hers.

"I know you're not. You got lost in a big way, but now it's up to you to find yourself again. You're a strong woman, Hailey. You always have been and you need to find that inner strength again."

"Thanks for believing in me, Collin. The first step in recovering is to be honest with myself and the people I love. The biggest mistake I ever made was breaking up with you, but I'm happy I did. You know why?"

I shook my head.

"Because our breakup led you to Amelia and she's a great girl. You better not screw things up with her." She smirked.

"I won't. You'll find someone too. You're a good person, Hailey. You just need to be a little more careful with the guys you choose." I gave her a wink.

She laughed. "I will. I promise. But to be honest, there won't be any more guys for a long time. I need to focus on me getting better and getting my career on track. That's my top priority. Everything else can wait."

"I'm proud of you."

"Friends?" she asked.

"Forever." I smiled.

"I hope one day you can forgive me for everything that happened when I left for Italy."

"You're already forgiven." I reached over and gave her a hug.

"Thanks, Collin. That means a lot to me."

"I better get home. Amelia's waiting for me. I asked her to come, but she thought that maybe we should talk alone."

"Tell her I said thank you for everything."

"You can tell her yourself when she comes to visit you. We'll stop by this weekend if that's okay with you?"

"I'd love that."

"Take care, Hailey," I said as I kissed her head.

"You too, Collin, and thanks for coming."

We walked back to the lobby, said goodbye, and she went back to her room. I climbed in the Range Rover and headed home to my wife. A feeling of contentment flowed through me knowing that Hailey was going to be all right.

# Chapter 37
## Connor

After my dinner with Lou, I went home and found Ellery taking a bath. I walked into the bathroom and she looked at me and smiled.

"Did you have a nice dinner with Lou?"

"Yeah. May I join you?" I asked as I pulled my shirt over my head.

"Of course."

She scooted up and I climbed in behind her, wrapping my arms around her silky smooth body as she rested her head against my chest.

"I need to talk to you about something."

"It's about Lucas, isn't it?"

"How did you know?"

"I'm your wife. I know you, Connor, and that dinner with Lou was about him, wasn't it?"

"Yes. His blood type is the same as Julia's. He lives in Vegas and I'm flying there tomorrow. Do you want to go with me?"

She softly kissed my arm. "I would love to go, but I think this is something you need to do on your own."

"Are you sure, baby?"

"I'm positive. You're not telling Julia, are you?"

"No. I'm not telling anyone. Not until I get some answers."

"Good."

"There's another thing I found out. Charlotte gave him our last name."

"Really? I'm surprised your father allowed that."

"I am too. I have a feeling there's a whole lot we don't know."

\*\*\*\*

I opened the door to the Presidential Suite at the Bellagio Hotel and the bellhop brought my luggage in.

"Enjoy your stay, Mr. Black, and it's nice to see you again." He smiled.

I reached into my pocket and pulled out a twenty-dollar bill. "Thank you, Ed. I intend to."

I unpacked my suitcase and pulled out the file folder that held the information about Lucas Black. I sighed as I stared at the address of his residence. I thought about calling him first, but I was sure he'd just hang up on me. So instead, I hired the same car service and driver I had for years drive me to his apartment. I made my way up to the second floor and found apartment 2D. Lightly knocking on the door, my nerves were running wild throughout my body. I stood there for a moment

*A Forever Family*

and waited for him to answer. But there was no answer. It was obvious he wasn't home. I turned around and headed down the hallway to the stairs. As I turned the corner, and pulled my phone from my pocket, I ran into someone. When I looked up, it was him. The six foot tall, sandy blonde, blue-eyed man that was the same person I spoke to at my father's funeral. His eyes widened when he saw me and he gulped. We both stood there for a moment in silence, neither one of us knowing what to say.

"Lucas?"

He began to walk away.

"I'm—"

"I know who you are, Connor. I don't know what you're doing here, but you need to leave and leave me alone." He headed down the hallway and I followed.

"Wait. Please. I know you're my brother."

He stopped but didn't turn around. "Just because we have the same blood running through us doesn't make us family." He walked to his apartment and inserted the key.

"I know he was an asshole. Believe me. But you were at his funeral. Why?"

"Because it's what my mother would have wanted. Now, if you'll excuse me." He opened the door.

"Lucas, I need to talk to you. Please. Will you just give me a chance? I'm sure it's what your mother would have wanted. For you to get to know your family."

The anger in his eyes erupted as he stood there and stared at me. "You have no right talking about my mother and I don't want to get to know any of you, especially if you're just like him." He walked in his apartment and shut the door.

*Shit.* I placed my hand on the back of my neck and sighed. How was I going to get him to talk to me and hear me out? I needed to devise a plan. A plan that would get his attention. I went back to the hotel and opened up the file on Lucas to see if there was anything else about him I could use to my advantage. Something interesting caught my attention. I pulled out my phone and dialed Ellery.

"Hello," she answered.

"Hi, baby."

"Did you talk to him?"

"Kind of. He pretty much slammed the door in my face. I need you to do me a favor."

"Anything, Connor."

"Apparently, he offers private cooking lessons on his nights off from the restaurant. I want you to call him and arrange a lesson. Tell him you're staying in the Presidential Suite at the Bellagio and give him your maiden name. Tell him he was recommended to you by a friend and you're only in Vegas for a short time."

I rattled off his phone number that was listed in the file and told her to call me back. About ten minutes later, my phone rang, and it was Ellery.

"Hey, baby."

"Your private cooking lesson is set for tomorrow night at six o'clock. It's a two-hour session and it's costing you $2,000. So pay attention because I want you to show me what you learned to prepare when you come home." She laughed.

"Thank you, Elle."

"You're welcome, darling. I miss you already."

"I miss you too, baby. I'll talk to you soon."

****

It was morning and I headed downstairs to the Café Bellagio for breakfast. As I was sipping my coffee and reading the *New York Times*, someone spoke to me.

"Excuse me, but you're one hell of a sexy man, and I'd love to have breakfast with you."

I looked up and a wide grin graced my face as I saw Ellery standing there.

"Baby, what are you doing here?" I got up from my seat, gave her a kiss, and pulled out the chair for her.

"I got to thinking last night that when you open the door to let Lucas in, he's might just bolt and that would be the end of that. So I decided to fly out here and give you a little help."

"You're amazing. I didn't even think of that."

"I figured that I would answer the door, let him get all set up, and then you could walk in, and I'd leave the two of you alone. I brought Peyton with me, so while you're getting to know your brother, we're going to do some gambling."

I sat there and shook my head at her. "I love you. Where is Peyton?"

"She's in her room lying down. She had one too many mimosas on the way here." She laughed. "I went up to the penthouse and, when there was no answer, I figured you'd be here eating breakfast. Now let me see that menu. I'm starving."

After enjoying a wonderful breakfast with my wife, we went up to the suite, made love, and then the three of us spent the day shopping and hanging out by the pool.

\*\*\*\*

## Ellery

We were sitting by the pool sipping margaritas when Peyton had a thought.

"You know, Elle. What if Lucas recognizes you from the funeral? In fact, if he already knew who Connor was, who's to say he doesn't know you."

"Shit, Peyton. I didn't think about that." I looked over at Connor and he sighed.

"No worries. I'll just pretend to be you. He wouldn't have clue who I am. You can wait for me down at the casino and when Connor makes his grand entrance, I'll meet you down there."

"Good idea, Peyton. I'm glad I brought you." I winked as I held up my glass to hers.

After enjoying the poolside, we headed upstairs to get ready for the evening.

"I'll be up to your suite around 5:30," Peyton said as she got off the elevator.

\*\*\*\*

*A Forever Family*

## Connor

Ellery left the suite and Peyton and I waited for Lucas to show up. I would be lying if I said I wasn't nervous. After our encounter yesterday, I was sure once he showed up, things were only going to get worse. There was a knock at the door and Peyton pushed me into the bedroom. Once she let him in, talked his ear off, and he got settled, I walked out of the room. He looked at me and slowly shook his head.

"What the fuck is going on here?" he asked in irritation.

I stood a few feet away from him with my hands in my pockets, studying his reaction.

"This was the only way to get you to meet me."

"No way, man." He began to pack up his things.

"Hold it right there, mister," Peyton said as she placed her hand up. "You aren't going anywhere. You're going to provide Connor with the service that he's paying you for. You're going to sit down and the two of you are going to talk whether you like it or not. You may not like each other, but you're going to hear one another out. You both share the same father and, from what I can tell, you are just as stubborn as he is." She pointed at me. "Now, I'm sorry, Lucas, that we had to trick you into coming here, but if you would have put your big boy pants on yesterday and just listened to Connor, we wouldn't be doing this right now. In fact, I'd be home cuddled up with my sexy husband, sipping champagne and eating chocolate-covered strawberries while he tells me about his long day at the hospital."

"Wait a minute. Aren't you his wife?" Lucas asked.

"No. I'm the best friend, Peyton. It's a pleasure to meet you." She held out her hand and he hesitantly shook it. "Now pop open a beer or have a scotch, in Connor's case, and talk like men do. If you'll excuse me, there's money to be won downstairs." She turned on her heels and walked out the door.

Lucas looked at me with a small smile. "I have to say, I'm kind of glad she's not your wife. She seems like a handful."

"You have no idea."

"Okay, Connor. You want to talk? So talk. But I'll warn you right now that I have nothing to say. I don't want to get to know the family that my father abandoned me and my mother for. Can you understand that?"

"I can, Lucas. I fully understand it. What is your preferred drink of choice?" I asked as I walked over to the bar.

"That Peyton chick said something about scotch. I like scotch."

"Me too. There's two things we have in common."

## Chapter 38
## Connor

"So, am I to assume you don't want a cooking lesson?" he asked.

I chuckled. "No. That's okay. I'll still pay you for your time." I handed him his scotch and took a seat in the black leather chair across from the couch.

"I'm on limited time here, so why don't you say what you have to say and we can go about our business."

As I sat back in the chair and stared at him, I realized that he reminded me so much of Collin. Not my son, but my twin brother. When I saw him at the funeral, his eyes were the first thing I noticed. I kept thinking that there was something about them that gripped me. Now that I was sitting across from him, I realized just what it was.

"I'm sorry about what our father did to you and your mother. He wasn't always a genuine caring man. He was a liar and a cheat."

"I came to terms with that a long time ago. See, the difference is I already knew about you and your sister. I obsessed over the fact that my father abandoned me. I came to terms that I would never be good enough for him, even though I carried his name. He had two other children that were more important and I was never allowed to become a part of that life. I was nothing but a secret; a bastard that would ruin his reputation if it ever got out that I existed."

The bitterness and anger that emerged from him was understandable. "I'm sorry, Lucas. All I can tell you is what you already know: he was an asshole. An asshole that the community worshiped. He put on an amazing façade. But I saw right through him."

"I am curious to know how you found out about me." He took a sip of his scotch.

"After he died, I was cleaning out his home office and found this picture." I pulled the picture from my pocket and handed it to him. "I knew that child wasn't me or Cassidy. I also found the purchase agreement for your house in Cherry Hill in a locked drawer of my father's desk. My son, Collin, and I took a ride there and that's when we met Flora. She told me everything."

"Ah, Flora." His lips gave way to a small smile. "She was like a grandmother to me. How is she?"

"She seemed well. She said that you moved away after your mother passed when you were eighteen."

He looked down and set his drink on the table as he got up from the couch. "Father paid me a visit the day of my mother's funeral. It was only the third time in my life that I'd seen him. He gave me his condolences and a check for one hundred thousand dollars to go start somewhere new because he was going to sell the house. He was afraid, now that my mother was gone, that I was going to come forth as his son. He made me

*A Forever Family*

sick standing there, pretending that he cared about my mother. I told him if he wanted me to go away, then he better up the offer to two hundred thousand and he'd never have to worry about me again."

I held up my glass to him. "I would have gone for more. But you did well."

"He gave it to me, I took it, and hopped on the next plane to Paris. I used the money to attend one of the finest culinary schools there. I studied, learned, and took odd jobs for about six years before moving back here and starting as a line cook at Sage. Because of my talent and what I learned in Paris, I was promoted to Executive Chef a couple of years later."

"Have you ever considered opening your own restaurant?" I asked.

"All the time. It's been a dream of mine since I was a kid. Unfortunately, opening a restaurant costs a lot of money, something I don't have. I don't want to open a cheap diner or nothing. I want to be the owner of a five-star restaurant."

His dreams were big and I liked that about him. He had ownership in his blood. I could help him make his dream come true if he'd help me, but I needed to be very careful with Lucas. I got the impression he was a ticking time bomb.

"I would like you to come and meet my family back in New York. Your family. You have a sister, niece, two nephews, and a great-nephew. And I know they'd want to meet you."

He took in a deep breath as he stared at me like he was prey and I was the great white shark, ready to strike.

"Thanks for the offer, Connor, but like I said earlier, I don't want to meet any more Blacks. You're lucky I even gave you the time I did. I know all about you, big brother. I've been watching you for years. You and your multibillion dollar company, Black Enterprises. A company that I should have some stake in, considering I'm one of the Black sons. But I was banished from your family. So go back to New York to your family, to your life and stay the fuck out of mine." He walked towards the door.

I stood up from my chair. "My daughter is ill and you're the only one who can help her," I yelled from across the room.

He stopped, slowly turned his head, and looked at me. The anger in his eyes grew.

"You didn't come here because you wanted to get to know me. You said earlier that you found the picture of me right after the funeral. That was three months ago. You never had any intention of finding me or else you would have done it then. You only came here out of desperation for your daughter."

"I was angry!" I yelled. "Angry at him and angry at you. I was pissed as hell that you existed because it reminded me just how much of a bastard he was! How he hurt my mother. He hurt both our mothers! You're my brother and you have a right to know your family!"

"I buried my family ten years ago. We're done here. I'm sorry about your daughter, but there's nothing I can do."

"You're throwing away the opportunity to own your restaurant. No cost is too great when it comes to my family. I can give you everything you need."

"Why can't you understand that I don't want anything from you? Just leave me alone. And the fact that you would try to buy me off makes you no better than him."

*A Forever Family*

"The Black men don't turn their backs on people in need!"

"Funny you should say that because I know one who did. Good bye, Connor." He walked out the door.

I picked up my glass from the table and threw it against the wall. He was my last hope for Julia.

## Chapter 39
## Ellery

When I came back to the suite last night, I found Connor sitting on the balcony, staring out into the brightly lit city. He was hurting and so was I when he told me the conversation he had with Lucas. My emotions were at an all-time high as I sat on his lap and we held each other, thinking about Julia.

"We're leaving Vegas tomorrow. There's no reason for us to be here anymore."

"What time?"

"The plane will be here around one."

"Peyton and I are going to do some shopping first thing in the morning. She wants to pick up a few things for Hailey."

"That's fine. Just make sure you're back in time."

"It's our plane, Connor. He's not going anywhere until we board."

"Ellery. It's not up for discussion. Do as I ask. Do you understand?"

His tone was stern, something I hadn't heard in a very long time, but I wasn't going to argue with him this time. The truth was I wasn't going shopping with Peyton. I was going to talk to Lucas and hopefully try to make him see things differently. I told Peyton my plan and made sure she stayed scarce while I was gone. Connor had left the file folder sitting on the dresser. While he was in the shower, I carefully opened it and typed Lucas's address into my phone. Climbing into bed and waiting for Connor to come out from the bathroom, I lay down as I devised my plan of action for tomorrow.

The next morning, I kissed Connor goodbye and told him that I'd be back in time for our flight back to New York. He insisted that he walk me and Peyton out the front doors of the hotel. As much as I loved him, sometimes he drove me nuts. As soon as Peyton and I climbed into the cab, she told the driver to drop her off a couple of blocks away as I rattled off Lucas's home address and told him to step on it. I didn't have much time.

Lightly knocking on the white painted door, I waited for a few moments before knocking harder. Suddenly, when I went to knock for the third time, the door flew open and Lucas stood there, staring at me, wearing pajama bottoms and messy hair. He reminded me so much of Connor when he was that age and it looked as though I had just woke him up.

"Can I help you?" he asked with sleepy eyes and a bit of an attitude.

"Actually, you can." I ducked underneath the arm that was holding the door open.

"Umm. Excuse me. Who do you think you are just barging into my apartment?"

"I'm Ellery Black." I turned and held out my hand to him and he walked away.

"I thought so. I saw you at the funeral and I've seen you in the papers with your husband."

"Your brother," I spoke.

"Like I told him before, just because we share the same blood doesn't make us family. I need some coffee and you need to leave."

Connor was right; he was angry, but there was a sadness I could see in his soul.

"You look hungover."

"That would be because I am and I have a killer headache. So if you'll excuse me, I need to go lie down."

When I walked into his tiny kitchen and opened the refrigerator, I smiled when I saw a majority of the ingredients I needed to make him the cocktail. He had all but two.

"What the hell do you think you're doing?" he asked in irritation. "You don't just go into someone's refrigerator like that, lady."

"Which neighbor is nicer? The one across the hall or next door?"

"What?" he asked in confusion.

I sighed. "Sit down. I'll be back in a second. Don't think about shutting your door either. Because I can make some pretty good noise and I'm sure you wouldn't want your neighbors to think you were having an affair with an older married woman."

He slowly sat down as he watched me prop the door open with a chair. I knocked on the door across the hall and an elderly woman answered. I told her that I was from across the hall and asked her if she had the two ingredients I was missing. She did and handed them over with a smile across her face. When I turned around and stepped back into the apartment, Lucas had his head down on the table.

"You're crazy. Do you know that?" His tone was muffled.

"Funny, because Connor tells me the same thing. Where's your blender?"

"Why do you need my blender? What the hell do you think you're doing? If I wasn't so hungover right now, I'd kick you right out of here."

"Then I guess it's lucky for me that you're hungover." I found the blender and put the ingredients in it. "Cover your ears; this is going to be loud."

Once everything was mixed, I poured it into a glass and sat down across from him, sliding the glass across the table.

"Drink up."

He picked up the glass, looked at it, and then brought it up to his nose. "What the fuck is this? You're crazy if you think I'm drinking this."

"It's a hangover cocktail and I promise you that you will start to feel better right after you drink it. I make it for Connor and Collin all the time. If you don't believe me, call him." I pulled out my phone and held it out to him.

He shot me a look as he brought the glass to his lips and drank the cocktail as fast as he could.

"Fuck! This is nasty stuff."

"That it may be, but you'll be thanking me in about fifteen minutes. Now, the reason I came to see you is to talk to you about your family."

He laid his head back down on the table. "I don't have a family. I already told your husband that and I just want to be left alone."

"I'm sure you do because then you can wallow in self-pity about how your father abandoned you. That is what you're doing, right?"

"You're wrong, Mrs. Black. You know nothing about me."

"You can call me Elle. That's what my friends call me."

"But we're not friends."

A small grin crossed my lips, because at that moment, I had flashbacks of my first dinner with Connor. They were more alike than they both wanted to admit.

"Let me tell you a little something about me. My mom passed away when I was a little girl. I was diagnosed with cancer at the age of sixteen and I tried to commit suicide. Hence the tattoos on my wrists to cover up the scars." I held out my wrists to him. "Then, when I was twenty three, I was diagnosed with cancer for a second time."

Lucas stared at me intently. "Two times at such a young age was too much to handle. There was no way I was going through chemo again, so I opted to let myself die. It was obvious to me that I wasn't meant to live a long life, so I decided to enjoy what little time I had left. My boyfriend of four years broke up with me over it and walked out of my life. Then I met Connor. I saw him getting thrown out of a club because he was too drunk. I put him in a cab and I helped him home. He's the reason I'm

*A Forever Family*

here today. Despite me keeping that I had cancer from him, he never once turned his back on me. No matter how pissed off and angry he was, and believe me, I thought he was going to kill me, he stood by my side. Even when I was so bitter and angry and did everything I could to push him away, he refused to leave."

I could tell he was feeling better because he no longer put his head on the table and he was sitting straight up. "So you ended up getting chemo?"

"I flew out to California and participated in a trial study for an extremely aggressive treatment and it worked and I've been in remission ever since. That was over twenty years ago."

"Congratulations, but I don't understand what your point is."

"My point is that things could have been a lot worse for you. I understand your feelings and I'm sorry my father in-law was such an asshole. But just because he was, doesn't mean that the rest of his family is. We Blacks help people no matter what and no matter the cost. You're a lot like Connor. I can tell and I also can tell that you're a good man. You're broken like he was when I first met him, and buried deep below that cocky piss-poor attitude and self-pity is a kind heart."

He got up from the table and took his glass to the kitchen. "I'm nothing like him. So stop thinking I am because it's really annoying."

"But you are, and if you would just get to know him, you'd see for yourself. I'm welcoming you to the family, Lucas, whether you like it or not. We are a very close knit family and we'd like for you to be a part of that."

"What's wrong with your kid?" he turned around and asked.

"Connor didn't tell you?"

"No. He just said she was sick."

"Julia and her husband were in a serious car accident a few months ago. The doctor had to remove one of her kidneys because it was severely damaged and her other kidney is failing."

"Wait a minute," he said as he pointed at me with his finger. "Are you asking me to give your kid one of my kidneys?"

"Yes. Yes I am."

"You're fucking crazy, lady. Oh my God," he said as he rubbed the back of his neck. "I can't believe the nerve of you people. And how do you know that I would even be a match?"

"What's your blood type?" I asked.

"Type O."

"So is Julia's."

He placed his hands on the kitchen counter and pushed back, straightening his arms. "You already knew that, didn't you?" he asked with a furrowed brow.

"Are you going to get pissed and start yelling if I tell you the truth?"

"Damn it!" He pushed off the counter. "I suppose Connor had me all checked out. Found out everything about me, including my fucking blood type. That's the only reason he came here. He wants something. My mother said that's what my father used to do before I was born. He'd disappear for a while but always came back when he wanted or needed something. He was a son of a bitch and your husband is no better!" he yelled as he slammed his fist on the counter.

I bolted up from the table and pointed my finger as I made my way over to him. "Don't you ever talk about my husband that way again! You don't even know him. He's nothing like his father and neither is anyone else in my family. Tell me something, Lucas. When you first found out about your father's other family, how did you feel?" I waited for his response as he looked down in anger. He didn't respond. "Tell me!" I demanded.

"I was pissed! I hated him for choosing them over me. I hated that I had to grow up an only child," he yelled as I could see the tears spring to his eyes. "I had a brother and a sister and I wasn't allowed to get to know them!"

"Exactly! And that's how Connor feels right now. He's pissed. Not at you but at his father. He needs time. You had years. He's only had a few months. You were in his position once. You felt what he's feeling now. The anger, the rage, and the hate that consumes you because of one person's actions. I'm here because you don't have to be alone anymore. You have a family that wants to meet you and get to know you."

He looked away. "You need to leave."

"I'm leaving, Lucas, and I'm sorry. I'm sorry for everything you went through and I'm sorry for us coming to Vegas. It was wrong and we never should have. Julia is our daughter and she's our world. We can't stand to see her suffer anymore. It's tearing Connor apart. Imagine if she was your daughter. I know you would stop at nothing to help her get better."

I grabbed my purse from the table and walked to the door. I placed my hand on the knob and turned around. "I hope you find what you're looking for, Lucas. You deserve closure and happiness."

## Chapter 40
## Collin

A couple of weeks had passed since my dad got back from Vegas and he was still acting weird. He told me it was because a business deal went sour, but I didn't believe him. I knew every business deal Black Enterprises was in negotiations with and from what I could find, not one of them had gone bad. I knew he was up to something and I was sure it involved Julia.

"Dad, can I come in?" I asked as I slowly opened his office door.

"Sure, son. Have a seat."

I walked over and took a seat, not caring what was about to come out of my mouth.

"What's up, Collin?"

"You've been a real asshole lately, Dad. I'm sorry, but I want to know what the hell is going on with you. I know you made up that story about the bad business deal and I want to know what's going on. Did you find a donor for Julia?"

His eyes diverted up at me as he threw his pen across the desk and leaned back in his chair.

"I thought I did, but he won't do it."

"Who?"

"Lucas. He's the same blood type as your sister."

"You talked to him?" I asked in shock.

"Yes. He lives in Las Vegas. He flat out said no and then called me a few choice words."

"Do you blame him, Dad? I mean, come on. You don't know him. He doesn't know you or Julia and you just show up one day and ask him for a kidney. To be honest, I'm surprised he didn't punch you."

He arched his brow. "Thanks a lot, son. Don't you dare tell your sister about this. Do you understand me?" His tone was authoritative.

As I got up from the chair, I sighed. "Yeah. I understand. I have a meeting to get to." Before walking out, I looked at him with sympathy. "You can't save the world, Dad. Some things just are the way they are. You can't fight every one's battle." He turned around and faced the window as I walked out of his office.

I was already running late for my meeting downtown, and Ralph was being occupied by my mom, so I hailed a cab. I climbed in and looked at my watch.

"Sorry, buddy, but you need to step on it. I can't be late for this meeting."

He nodded his head and gave me a small smile through his rearview mirror. I sat back and checked my phone as he moved in and out of traffic with finesse. He didn't drive like the normal cab drivers of New York City. He drove with precision and seemed to glide on the streets of New York like a swan glides gracefully across the water.

"How long have you been driving?"

"About ten years now. I just moved here last month from L.A."

"So you're used to this kind of traffic." I smiled.

"Yeah. I am. The family I used to drive for back in L.A. split up. He went to prison for embezzlement and the IRS took everything they had. Needless to say, they didn't need a driver anymore."

Now he had really caught my attention. "What's your name?"

"Tommy. Tommy Johnson."

"Nice to meet you, Tommy. I'm Collin Black."

He looked at me through his rearview mirror. "I know who you are, Mr. Black, and it's nice to meet you."

He pulled up to the curb of the Waldorf where the meeting I was attending was being held in one of the conference rooms. I pulled some cash from my pocket and paid the fare, then looked at my watch.

"You got me here with five minutes to spare. Thank you, Tommy. How would you like to work for me as my personal driver?"

"Seriously, Mr. Black?"

"Yes. I've been looking for one for a long time and no one seemed right. But for some reason, you do. Here's my business card. Come by my office tomorrow morning around ten o'clock and we can discuss the details of your employment. That is, if you're interested?"

"Why, yes. Of course I'm interested."

"Great. I'll see you tomorrow." I smiled as I shut the door and strutted into the Waldorf. Jackpot! I finally found myself a driver and I couldn't wait to tell Amelia.

*A Forever Family*

## Chapter 41
## Connor

I took Julia to her dialysis appointment and spent a couple of hours with her before I had to attend a meeting at work. Jake was at the office and, as soon as I got back, he was going to spend the rest of the day with Julia. I took hold of her hand and brought it up to my lips.

"How are you doing, princess?"

"I'm okay, Dad. Listen, you don't need to be here. You're so busy at work and I'm fine."

"Collin can handle the company. The way I look at it is, this is some good father/daughter bonding time. We really don't get to spend any time alone together."

"I talked to the doctor and I'm thinking about doing dialysis at home. Jake and I talked about it and we think it would be better and more manageable."

My heart sank at the thought. It would be more manageable for her, but it would also seem more permanent, and it saddened me that there was nothing I could do. Actually, there was something I could do, but I made a promise to Julia that I wouldn't get involved and I'd never broken a promise to my daughter.

After a couple of hours had passed, Jake walked into the room. I gave Julia a kiss on her forehead and headed to the office.

"Good bye, princess." I winked.

"Bye, Dad." She smiled.

\*\*\*\*

## Julia

I kissed Jake goodbye before he left for work and took Brayden back to bed with me. I took the next couple of days off because the exhaustion was overwhelming. In a few days, I would start in-home dialysis and I was thrilled. Not thrilled about the dialysis part, but thrilled that I could do it in the comfort of my own home. After Brayden and I slept for a couple of hours, I decided to take him to Central Park since it was a beautiful day. He loved it there because he loved to be outside. I didn't tell anyone in my family that I was going because I just wanted to spend some time alone with my son. I packed the diaper bag, put Brayden in his stroller, and headed to Central Park.

I found a spot in the plush grass, spread out a blanket, and took Brayden from his stroller, setting him down amongst some of the toys I brought. The sky was clear and the sun was shining brightly. It was a warmer than usual day for this time of the year and, for the first time in a long time, it felt peaceful. As Brayden was playing with his toys, I pulled my ringing phone from my purse.

## A Forever Family

"Hey, Collin."

"Hey, sis. What are you doing?"

*Shit.* If I told him where I was, he'd want to come.

"I just put Brayden down for a nap and I'm going to lie down for a while."

"Oh. I was going to see if you wanted to grab some lunch."

"Maybe another time, Collin."

"Are you feeling okay, sis?"

"I'm fine. Just a little tired."

"Okay. Get some rest. I'll talk to you later."

I felt bad for lying to him, but I just wanted to be alone in the park with my son. If I would have told him I was here, he would have told my dad, who would have called my mom, and the three of them would have shown up. As much as I loved my family to death, I just needed some time alone. An hour passed, and as I fed Brayden his bottle, he fell asleep. I adjusted his stroller seat and laid him down so he could sleep comfortably. Bringing my knees up to my chest, I looked around the park at all the people who were there relaxing, sunbathing, exercising, and just enjoying the beautiful day. I noticed a man jogging by and suddenly, he collapsed to the ground, falling to his knees. I got up and ran over to him, taking hold of his arm.

"Are you okay?" I asked.

He turned his head and looked at me while trying to catch his breath.

"Thanks. I'm fine. I think I just need some water."

"I have plenty of water over here. Come with me." I helped him up and took a bottle of water from the small cooler I had brought. "Here, drink this."

"Thanks." He gave a small smile as he opened the water and took a sip.

"You shouldn't be running on this warm day with no water. Please sit down and rest until you're hydrated."

He sat down on the blanket and thanked me. "I left my wallet at home and I didn't realize it until I went to buy a bottle of water."

He finished the bottle and I handed him another one. "Drink up." I smiled.

"Thank you. Is that your baby?" He pointed to the stroller.

"Yeah. That's Brayden. He's my world." I yawned.

"Am I boring you?" He chuckled.

"Oh my God, no. I'm so sorry. I'm just really tired. I've had a major life change recently and it's really taken its toll on me."

"I'm sorry. Do you mind if I ask what happened? That was rude. I'm a complete stranger and I shouldn't have asked that."

He was right. I didn't even know his name, but that was okay. There was something about him that made me feel comfortable. I couldn't tell you what, but it was just something I'd felt.

"Sometimes talking to a complete stranger is the easiest. I was in a car accident a few months ago and both my kidneys were severely damaged. The doctors had to remove one of them and, as for the other, I'm on dialysis."

"I'm sorry."

"Thank you. I'm trying to adjust but between the exhaustion and the other effects from it, I just feel crappy all the time. I think a lot of it is depression as well. I put on this brave front for my family, especially my husband, because I know how bad this is hurting him to see me go through this. But on the inside, I'm a total mess."

Brayden woke up and started to fuss. "Excuse me a moment," I said as I got up and took him from his stroller. "Not too long ago, I was hospitalized with a bacterial infection and couldn't see him for a few days. I think that was the absolute worst thing I ever had to do. A woman came forth and she was going to donate one of her kidneys. Once all the initial workup was done and everything was all set, she got a call from the lab saying they thought they had made an error and asked her to come back in to be retested. It turned out she had cancer, so she could no longer be a donor."

"Wow. How unlucky for her and you. You must have been devastated," he spoke as he looked at Brayden and lightly touched his hand.

"To say the least. It felt like my whole world came crumbling down once again." Brayden was smiling at the stranger and cooing. "He seems to like you." I smiled.

"He seems like a great kid."

"He is and sometimes—" I looked down as tears started to form in my eyes. I set Brayden down on the blanket and handed him a toy before gently wiping away the tear. "Sometimes the thought of not being here for him scares me."

"You're not dying."

"I will if I stop the dialysis. He has his whole life ahead of him. There will be little league, music lessons, art classes, and school. How am I going to be able to keep up with all that? I can barely manage life now. I'm sorry," I spoke as I wiped another tear away.

"Please don't apologize. I'm so sorry you're going through this. You seem like such a nice woman and this just isn't fair. You said you were putting on a brave front for your family. How are they doing with all of this?"

Brayden started to fuss, so I grabbed a bottle from the diaper bag and gave it to him. "My family is destroyed about it, especially my dad. He and I are very close and I see how much this is killing him every time I look in his eyes. He wants to help me so badly, but he can't. My mom is being overprotective and my brother is putting on a brave front for me. But I can see right through him."

"I can imagine that there's nothing your father can do," he spoke.

"He's been through so much in his life with my mom having cancer before I was born and not knowing if her experimental treatments were going to work. Then he had an issue with a woman who stalked him. She burnt down his office building in Chicago and then tried to hurt my mom."

"Are you serious?" he asked with surprise.

"Yeah. Then his driver, who was like a father to him, passed away several months ago, and he took that very hard. In fact, he's still trying to cope with it. Then his own father passed away recently and he just found out that his father had an affair with a woman and they had a child together. A child that was kept secret from the family. I can't believe I just told you all that."

He softly placed his hand on my arm. "Like you said earlier, sometimes talking to a total stranger is easy. Sounds like your dad has been through the ringer."

"He has, and now with what I'm going through, he feels helpless and I hate seeing him like that. He's a good man and a very giving man. If you need help, he won't even hesitate. My brother, Collin, met a woman and her very sick son on a plane to Chicago. Her husband had passed away and she lost her job. She spent what little savings she had for her son's medical care."

"What's wrong with him?"

"He has cystic fibrosis. When my brother told my dad about their situation, he hired her as his secretary and gave her full health benefits so she didn't have to worry about her son's medical bills anymore. Then, when he was getting worse by living in the city, my dad moved her and Jacob to California and is letting them live in our beach house there and gave her a job at the art gallery he and my mom own."

"Why California?"

"The saltwater and ocean air helps Jacob's lungs and he's doing much better there. We just saw them at my grandfather's funeral and at my brother's wedding reception. He's doing really well. I'm so sorry. I must be boring you to death." I gave a small smile.

"Not at all. Your family sounds like they're really caring people."

"They are." I looked at my watch and noticed the time. "I better get Brayden home. My husband will be home soon."

I picked up Brayden and sat him in his stroller. "I'm sorry, I never asked you your name."

He smiled as he folded the blanket for me. "If I told you my name, then we would no longer be strangers and maybe you'd regret telling me everything you did."

"You're right. It was nice talking to you, stranger."

"The pleasure was mine, stranger. Thank you again for your help. Obviously, it runs in the family."

"You're welcome. Next time, make sure you have water on you." I pushed the stroller and headed home.

As much as I wanted to be alone, I found comfort in talking to the man who had collapsed in front of me. It felt good to tell someone my story. I decided not to tell Jake or anyone in the family about my encounter with the stranger. It was a moment that made my day a little better.

## Chapter 42
## Connor

I was sitting in my office when Collin walked in.

"Hey, Dad. Guess what?" he said happily.

"What's up, son? I'm really busy at the moment."

"I've hired a driver and I wanted to share the good news."

I looked up from my computer. "That's great. Where did you find him?"

"In a cab yesterday. He's from California and he drove for a couple there. He can weave in and out of this godforsaken traffic like nobody's business."

"Why is he here in New York? What happened with his last job?"

"The guy went to prison for embezzlement and the IRS took everything from him and the wife. He's originally from New York, so he thought it would be good idea to move back here."

"I'm happy for you, son. We can talk more about it over family dinner tonight. Right now, I have to get these contracts done."

"Okay. I'll see you later, Dad."

I gave him a smile as he walked out of my office. Looking back at my computer, I didn't hear the door shut. Instead, I heard a voice from the doorway.

"Fancy office you have here, big brother."

I looked up and stared at Lucas as he stood across the room. "Lucas. What are you doing here?" I got up from my chair.

"No need to get up, Connor. May I?" he asked as he pointed to the chair across from my desk.

"Sure. Please sit down."

He took a seat and continued to look around my office.

"Can I get you something to drink? A scotch, perhaps?"

"Yeah. I could use one about now." He slowly nodded his head.

I walked over to the bar and poured us each a drink. When I handed it to him, he thanked me and took a sip.

"Maybe I was wrong about you," he said.

"Why?" I asked with suspicion.

"Just some things I'd heard. Listen, I've been doing some thinking and maybe I can help Julia out."

My heart started to race. Was he joking? What the fuck was going on?

"Are you serious or is this some kind of joke?"

"It's no joke, Connor. I want to help Julia."

*A Forever Family*

"Why? What made you change your mind?"

"Your wife can be quite persuasive."

"What are you talking about? How do you know Ellery?"

He cocked his head and raised his brow. "She didn't tell you?"

"Tell me what?"

"She paid me a little visit the next morning after you and I had our little talk. She just barged into my apartment like she owned the place and refused to leave."

I chuckled. "Yep. That's my wife."

"I was hungover as shit because I stopped at the bar after we talked and I drank way too much. She made herself at home in my kitchen and made me drink this horrible-tasting shit after she went to my neighbor's apartment across the hall and asked for a couple of ingredients so she could make it."

I let out a laugh. "She's been shoving that shit down my throat from the first day we met. I met her in my kitchen, making the same thing. But you have to admit that it works."

"Yeah. It sure does." He smiled. "She told me about herself and what she'd been through and how you never turned your back on her."

"How much did she tell you?"

"A lot. Enough to make me want to fly here and meet your daughter to see for myself if you're all really as great as everyone claims you are."

"And?" I asked.

"I talked to Julia yesterday in Central Park, but she doesn't know it was me."

I shook my head. "What? Wait a minute. I don't understand."

"I followed her to Central Park and pretended to collapse in front of her. She helped me, gave me a couple bottles of water, and we sat and talked. She told me about her accident, her being on dialysis, her husband, and she talked a lot about you. You have one hell of a daughter, Connor, and I can easily say that I'm proud she's my niece."

"Why would Julia do that? Why would she tell you all that?"

"Because she's hurting and she said it's easier to talk to a complete stranger sometimes. She's putting on a front for all of you. She's not okay, but I want to change that for her. She told me about what you did for that kid and his mom."

"I see."

"That was really cool of you, and after hearing Ellery's story, you're nothing like our father. In fact, she told me about your driver that recently passed away. She said he was like a father to you. Why?"

I leaned back in my chair and took a sip of my scotch. "Denny was a amazing man. He was there for me through every bad and good thing I encountered in life. He was there when our father wasn't. He helped me through some really tough times and he was a great man and my best friend."

Lucas glared at me and narrowed his eyes. "Denny?"

"Yes."

"I met him a couple of times. He would come by the house and drop off packages for us. One night, I was sitting on the porch because my mom was in the house crying over something Dad had said to her over the phone and he happened to stop by. He asked me where my mom was and I told him she was in the house crying. It really made me sad to see her so unhappy. He sat down on the porch next to me and I'll never forget what he said."

"What did he say?"

"He said, 'Son, never let the circumstances in life get in your way of becoming a great man. Shit happens and sometimes life isn't fair, but you were made to be someone special and no matter what happens, you need to follow what's in your heart. Don't become a victim of circumstances.'"

Tears started to fill my eyes as did his. "That sounds like something he'd say."

"I never saw him again after that, but I never forgot him."

A moment of silence overtook the room. "Family dinner is tonight. Please join us at my penthouse and meet the rest of your family. Julia and Jake will be there and so will Collin and Amelia. You can tell Julia yourself that you want to help her."

"Thank you, Connor. I'd love to meet the rest of my family. I just hope Julia doesn't get mad at me when she finds out what I did yesterday."

"She won't. She's a great woman and she'll understand why you did it."

"She is a great woman. You're very lucky to have two wonderful women in your life. That wife of yours is quite a spitfire." He laughed.

I sighed. "Tell me about it."

"I'm really shocked she didn't tell you that she came to see me."

"Believe me, Lucas. It doesn't shock me at all. If there's one thing Elle is good at, it's keeping secrets."

He chuckled. "What time tonight?" he asked as he got up from his chair.

"Dinner is at seven o'clock and don't be late. Ellery hates it when people are late."

"Are you going to tell her I'm coming?"

"Nah. Let's surprise her." I smiled. I wrote my address and phone number on the pad of paper in front of me, ripped it off, and handed it to him. "Here's my phone number and address. Remember, seven sharp."

"Believe me, I won't be late."

As he headed towards the door, I stopped him.

"Hey, Lucas?"

"Yeah." He turned around.

"Thank you."

"No problem, bro. I'll see you tonight."

I couldn't describe the feeling of happiness that overtook me. This was nothing short of a miracle and I couldn't believe it. I pressed the intercom button.

"Yes, Connor?" Laurinda asked.

## A Forever Family

"You know what? Forget it, Laurinda. I was going to have you do something, but I'm going to do it myself."

I shut down my computer because the work could wait. As far as I was concerned, this night was more important. I grabbed my briefcase, left the office, and had Ralph drive me to the florist.

"Good day, Mr. Black. How can I help you?" Sally, the sales associate asked.

"I need three dozen roses. Red for my wife and pink for my daughter and daughter-in-law."

"Coming right up." She smiled.

A few moments later, Sally returned with three dozen beautifully arranged and wrapped roses.

"Thank you, Sally. Have a great night."

"You too, Mr. Black."

****

I stepped off the elevator and walked into the kitchen, looking for Ellery. She wasn't in there. I set the roses down and headed upstairs. When I walked into the bedroom, I heard the shower running. I stripped out of my clothes, walked into the bathroom, and opened the shower door. Ellery jumped.

"Fuck! You scared the shit of out me."

"Sorry, baby. I wanted to surprise you." I ran my hands lightly over her beautiful breasts.

"What are you doing home already?"

"I came home to fuck you."

A smile crossed her lips as she placed her hand on my bare chest. "Hmm. What if I don't want to be fucked, Mr. Black?"

"Nonsense. Now stop asking questions and turn around."

She did as I asked and placed her hands against the marble wall. My fingers slipped inside of her as my other hand groped her breast. She moaned as my lips traveled across her neck, lightly nipping her wet, delicate skin. I was rock hard and I couldn't wait to be inside of her.

"Spread your legs, baby," I whispered as I tugged at her hard nipple while the hot water beaded down on us.

I thrust myself inside, pushing into her and burying my cock so deep that the sensation overwhelmed us. As I rapidly moved in and out of her, she moaned with each deep thrust. I pulled out and turned her around, bringing her legs up around my waist as she wrapped them tightly around me and I held her up firmly by her perfect ass. I continued to thrust in and out of her rapidly, feeling the warmth of her come explode all over my cock. Her moans heightened as she dug her nails into my back. One last deep thrust was all it took as I spilled every drop of pleasure I had inside of me into her. I looked into her eyes. The eyes of the love of my life and I smiled.

"I love you so much, baby."

"I love you too." She smiled back as she gently brushed her lips against mine.

## Chapter 43
### Connor

After we got dressed, we went downstairs and I handed Ellery her roses.

"What are these for?"

"No reason. Do I need a reason to give my beautiful wife roses?"

"No. Thank you. I love them and best of all, they're not black."

"You're welcome." I kissed her. "These are for Julia and Amelia. We better get them in some water."

Ellery walked to the cabinet and took out three vases.

"You need to set an extra place at the dinner table," I spoke.

"Oh really? Who's coming?"

"I invited a friend for dinner."

"Which friend?"

"You'll see." I winked and proceeded to walk to the living room.

Before she could question me, the elevator doors opened and Julia, Jake, and Brayden stepped off.

"Hi, princess." I walked over and kissed her cheek. I shook Jake's hand and took my grandson from his arms, giving him a big kiss.

Not too long after, Collin and Amelia showed up and I handed both her and Julia their flowers.

"Beautiful flowers for beautiful women."

"Thank you, Daddy." Julia smiled.

"Thank you, Dad." Amelia kissed my cheek.

I looked at my watch and it was six fifty. Lucas was going to be here any minute, so I gathered everyone into the living room. The elevator doors opened and I stepped into the foyer while everyone was chatting.

"Welcome, Lucas." I smiled as I shook his hand.

"Thanks, Connor. I will admit that I'm a little nervous."

"Don't be."

I led him into the living room and silence filled the air as everyone stopped talking and stared at us.

"I would like you all to meet my brother, Lucas."

Ellery walked over and placed her hands on each side of his face with a smile. "Welcome to our home."

"Thank you, Elle." He smiled back.

Julia got up from the couch and walked over to him. "I—I—"

## A Forever Family

"I'm sorry I didn't tell you who I was yesterday, Julia. I had my reasons."

She wrapped her arms around him and gave him a hug. "I knew there was something special about you."

"What's going on?" Collin asked.

I introduced Collin, Jake, and Amelia to Lucas and he explained what happened yesterday in Central Park. I walked over to Ellery, placed my hand on her hip, and whispered in her ear.

"We will talk about a little conversation you neglected to tell me about."

She looked at me with a cocky smile. "Be quiet, Connor."

I chuckled and we all went into the dining room for dinner. We spent the next couple of hours laughing, talking, and getting to know Lucas better. Collin looked at me from across the table with a smile and gave me a wink. It was a wonderful night in the Black household and everyone was happy.

After dinner, we all went back into the living room and Lucas sat down next to Julia, taking hold of her hand.

"Julia, I've given this a lot of thought and I'm going to donate one of my kidneys to you."

"What? How? You don't—"

"My blood type is O and as long as everything else is okay, my kidney belongs to you."

Tears started to stream down her face as she covered her mouth with her hands.

"You're a very special woman and that little boy of yours is going to have a healthy mom for the rest of his life."

She began to cry and wrapped her arms around him. "I don't know what to say. I'm speechless."

"I think we're all speechless, sis," Collin spoke. "Lucas, you are one special dude. Welcome to the family, man."

"Thanks, Collin. Someone once told me that the Blacks never turn their back on someone in need. Julia, just tell me what I need to do. I've decided to move to New York, so I'll be sticking around."

"What about your job at Sage?" I asked.

"I quit. There are plenty of high end restaurants here in New York that I can work for."

"Where are you staying?" Ellery asked.

"I got a room at the Hilton."

"Nonsense, you're staying with us until you find a permanent place."

"Thanks, Elle, but that's okay."

She shot him a look and he looked at me. I lightly shook my head at Lucas.

"Okay. If you insist." He smiled.

"That's better. I'm going upstairs to get your room ready. Amelia, could you please help me?"

Collin walked over to where Lucas was sitting. "You're already learning that nobody tells my mom no."

He chuckled. "She kind of scares me, to be honest."

"She scares all of us." I laughed.

"I heard that, Connor!" she yelled from upstairs.

## Chapter 44
### Julia

Over the next week, Lucas did all the workup that was necessary and he was a perfect match. Dr. Benson was thrilled and scheduled the surgery for tomorrow morning. I was scared shitless, to say the least, but I had my husband and my family by my side. Jake and I took Lucas to dinner alone, while my mom and dad watched Brayden for us. Lucas promised to show me how to make some wonderful dishes once we recovered from our surgery. He was a godsend to me and I couldn't stop thinking about what Denny had told me that night of the accident and how everything happens for a reason. I knew he was watching over us and I was no longer scared of what was to come. This man, my uncle that I'd only known for a little over a week, was the one who was sent to save my life. He was doing something so selfless and I'd spend the rest of my life thanking him.

As I lay in the hospital bed with Jake by my side, waiting for them to transport me to the operating room, my dad walked in and took hold of my hand.

"This is it, princess." He smiled tenderly at me.

"It sure is, Dad. Thank you for everything. I can't believe this is actually happening."

*A Forever Family*

"Are you scared?"

"Just a little, but I know that Denny will be watching over me."

"If you see that old man, tell him I said thanks." He leaned down and kissed my forehead.

My mom walked over and my dad went to see Lucas.

"We'll be here waiting for you when you wake up, sweetheart. We're all here for you and for Lucas."

"Thanks, Mom. Thank you for everything you've done."

The nurses walked into the room. "The team is ready for you, Julia."

My mom leaned down and kissed my head. "Good luck, baby girl."

Jake brushed his lips against mine before they wheeled me out of the room. "I love you, Julia."

"I love you more, Jake."

As they wheeled me into the operating room, Lucas was already in there. The nurse transferred me to the operating table and I extended my hand to him.

"This is it." He smiled.

"Yeah. This is it. Thank you again."

"Don't mention it. It's only a kidney. No big deal." He winked.

That was the last thing I remembered before drifting off into a peaceful sleep.

## Chapter 45
## Connor

*Two Months Later...*

Julia's transplant went well and her body accepted Lucas's kidney without any complications. Both patients were doing good and Julia was starting to get back to her normal self. Cassidy and Lucas were getting to know each other better and the three of us had dinner together at least once a week. My mother couldn't bring herself to meet Lucas yet. She said she needed time. Collin and Lucas were growing close and it made me happy to have him as part of our family. We put our past with our father behind us and concentrated on the future.

I stood outside a building on East 76th Street and waited for Lucas to meet me. When the taxi pulled up, he got out and looked at the building.

"So why are we meeting here?" he asked.

"I want to show you something. Follow me."

I opened the large wooden doors and we walked inside. "What do you think of this place?" I asked.

"It's cool. But I don't understand. There's nothing here."

*A Forever Family*

"There will be if you're interested." I smiled.

He narrowed his eye at me. "What do you mean, Connor?"

"Take a look around at your new restaurant, Lucas."

"No way. No way! Connor, I can't let you do this."

"Sure you can. It's yours. I bought the building for you to turn it into anything you want. See, we Black men own our own businesses. We don't work for anyone. They work for us."

"I can't believe this," he said in excitement as he placed his hands on his head. "I just can't accept this. It's not right."

"It's totally right, little brother. I'll charge you a monthly rent for the building. Other than that, everything else is yours. This is your restaurant. Turn it into your dream. You deserve it. You can consider me a silent partner if you want. I have a crew who is ready to go over the plans with you to help you get started."

"I don't know what to say. I can't believe this. Thank you," he said as he gave me a light hug.

"You're welcome. What do you think you want to call this place?"

"Julia's. Do you think she'll mind?"

I hooked my arm around him. "I don't think she'll mind at all." I smiled.

"I need to get my own place. As much as I like living with you and Elle, I need my own bachelor pad."

"Ellery will be upset. She'll miss your cooking."

"She'll be okay."

"Are you going to tell her that?" I chuckled.

"I was hoping you would." He laughed.

****

## Collin

Amelia was in the bathroom as I waited nervously on the edge of the bed for her to come out.

"Well, I took it. Now we wait," she said as she sat down next to me.

I put my arm around her and pulled her into me, kissing the side of her head.

"If it's positive, it'll be a good thing, right? If it's negative, that would be good too."

She sighed as she laid her head on my shoulder. "Both would be okay. I know we didn't plan on having kids this soon, but if it's meant to be, it's meant to be. I just don't know if I'm ready to be a mom yet."

"I'm not sure I'm ready to be a dad yet either."

"I just started my career," she spoke.

"We just started our marriage. I would have liked some more time alone before we brought a baby into our family."

The timer on her phone went off and we both looked at each other nervously. "You go look," she said.

"No. You go look."

*A Forever Family*

"Fine. We'll look together." She got up from the bed and grabbed my hand. When we walked into the bathroom, we both closed our eyes.

"Okay. I have it in my hand. On the count of three, we'll find out if we're going to have a baby. One. Two. Three!" We both opened our eyes and looked at the white stick Amelia held in her hand. We both let out a sigh of relief and at the same time spoke, "Oh thank God."

She set the stick down and I wrapped my arms around her tightly. "It wouldn't have been so bad if it was positive."

"No, it wouldn't have. But it's not and I'm okay with that."

I broke our embrace and placed my hands on each side of her face. "Me too. We have plenty of time to start a family." I softly brushed my lips against hers.

## Chapter 46
## Ellery

*Six Months Later…*

The holidays had come and gone and they were celebrated with such joy. Having Lucas here with us, his family, was the best thing that could have happened to us. The opening of his restaurant was in a couple of days and we were so excited for him. Julia was back to her normal self and now that Brayden had started walking, he kept her and all of us on our toes.

I went to Black Enterprises to have lunch with Connor. After speaking with Ethan and Laurinda for a bit, I walked into his office and found him staring out the window.

"Lunch has arrived," I said as I held up the brown bag.

He turned around and smiled. "So has my beautiful wife." He turned his chair around, got up and walked over and gave me a kiss.

I wiped the lipstick from his lips with my thumb. "Are you okay? You looked like you were in deep thought."

"I've made the decision to hand over the company to Collin and Julia effective thirty days from today."

## A Forever Family

My eyes widened. "What? Are you sure?"

He took the brown bag from me and set it on his desk. Taking the sandwiches from it, we sat down at the round table in his office.

"It's time, Elle. It's time I retire and let the kids take over. Just like my father did for me. With Julia back to herself and Collin's superb business skills and knowledge, I don't see why I should put it off any longer."

"That's wonderful, Connor. When are you going to tell them?"

"I'm planning on telling them next week."

"They're going to be so thrilled. I know this must be somewhat difficult for you."

"Not really. It'll be weird not coming to the office every day, but it's all the more time I get to spend with you." He took hold of my hand and brought it up to his lips.

I gave him a warm smile. "This makes me very happy, Mr. Black. We've waited for this day for a long time."

"We sure have, baby. Start figuring out where you want to go for our first vacation."

"I've already been thinking about that and I'd love to go to Spain. We've never been there."

"Spain it is, baby. Now, it's just you and me taking on the world." He winked. "Oh, by the way, we're flying to California next week. There's some business I need to take care of there with the art gallery."

"Oh great. We can see Diana and Jacob, Mason and Landon, and Ian and Rory." I smiled. "Mason will be thrilled that we're coming."

****

# Connor

The opening of Julia's was a huge success. Lucas had done an amazing job with the restaurant and the food critics were already leaving five-star reviews in the food and entertainment section of all the major newspapers. Lucas was a true Black and I couldn't be happier. Emotions were running high that night as I hugged and congratulated him on a job well done.

"Congratulations, little brother. You deserve all of this."

"Thanks, Connor. None of this would have been possible without you."

"Nah. I just provided the building. You did everything else. Look at this place. It's amazing and look at all the people who have come here to eat your food."

Peyton, Henry, and Hailey walked through the door and I gave Lucas a pat on the back. "Peyton and Henry are here."

We walked over to them and I gave them each a light hug. Looking at Hailey, I took hold of both her hands and gave her a warm smile.

"How are you, sweetheart?"

"I'm good, Connor. Really good, in fact. I've never been better, to be honest."

"I'm happy to hear that."

*A Forever Family*

"Lucas, I would like you to meet, Hailey, Peyton and Henry's daughter."

Both of them stood there for a moment and stared at each other. I looked over at Henry and he gave me an odd look. He knew just as well as I did what their stares meant.

"It's very nice to meet you, Hailey," Lucas spoke as he smiled brightly at her.

"It's nice to meet you too, Lucas. This place is amazing. Congratulations."

"Thank you. Would you like a tour?"

"Of course."

The two of them walked away and I hooked my arm around Henry. "You saw it too?" I asked.

"Yep. I sure did. That was the look of love at first sight."

I chuckled. "Come on; let's get a drink."

## Chapter 47
## Connor

Ellery and I boarded the plane for California and took our seats in first class.

"I still don't understand why you couldn't have the plane fixed sooner."

"I already told you Elle, that the mechanics were waiting for a part to come in. There's nothing wrong with flying commercial."

"No. There's not. But I like our private plane."

"Have a drink. You'll be fine." I smiled.

I was minding my own business when Ellery tapped me on the shoulder. I looked over at her and she had that look on her face, the one that she got when she was getting ready to tell someone off.

"What's wrong?"

"Can we switch seats, please?"

"Why? You love sitting by the window."

"Not today I don't."

I got up from my seat and we switched. I didn't understand what the hell was going on and why she wanted to switch. She sat down in the aisle seat and I watched her as she looked at the attractive young woman sitting in the seat across the aisle from her. Nervousness was settling through me because I just knew she was going to say something to her. I wasn't completely oblivious to the woman staring at me and certainly not when she dropped her napkin, got up from her seat, and bent down in the middle of the aisle to pick it up, making sure I took note of her cleavage. Oh boy. I braced myself as the woman gave Ellery a dirty look.

"Oh, I'm sorry. Did I disrupt your annoying little staring act at my husband? I can guarantee that I'm just as good." She winked at her.

"I don't know what you're talking about. I wasn't staring at him."

"Yes, you were. You had your eyes locked on him at the gate even before we got on the plane. What were you hoping to accomplish by your little napkin trick? You can clearly see that he's married by the wedding band he's wearing."

I placed my hand on Ellery's arm. "Elle, that's enough," I whispered.

She ignored me.

"I know he's probably the best eye candy you've ever seen, but it's very rude to stare. Didn't your mother ever teach you any manners?"

I rested my head on my hand and closed my eyes.

"I'm sorry. I didn't mean to—"

"Yes, you did. But now, you'll have the pleasure of staring at me." Ellery smiled. "Word of advice because you're still young. Imagine if someone did that to your husband. You wouldn't be happy about it. Our men are our men and we don't appreciate other woman gawking at them. Am I clear?"

"Yes. You've made yourself very clear." She turned her head.

Ellery turned to me and grabbed my hand. "You're the one who made us fly commercial. You knew the risk, Connor. You knew the risk."

I sighed as I stared out the window.

****

# Ellery

We stayed with Diana and Jacob at the beach house. It was so good to see them again. Mason and Landon met us there and we had a couple of drinks.

"Come on, Elle. We're going out."

"Where are we going?"

"You'll see."

"Isn't that kind of rude just to up and leave our friends?"

"No. It's not rude at all. Now get in the limo," he commanded.

"You're awful bossy, Mr. Black."

He chuckled as he pulled a black tie from his pocket and put it around my eyes.

"What are you doing?" I asked.

"It's a surprise and I don't want you to see until we get there."

I bit down on my bottom lip in anticipation. We drove for a bit and then the limo stopped. Connor opened the door and took my hand, helping me out of the car. I could smell the ocean air and I could hear the waves crashing against the shore. He stopped and bent down and took off my shoes. He picked me up and carried me a few feet before setting me down in the warm sand and taking off the blindfold.

"Recognize this place?" he asked.

"It's the beach where you proposed to me. I could never forget this place." I smiled as we walked to the shore hand in hand. "What are we doing here?"

Connor stopped and took hold of both my hands. "I wanted to make this place special for a second time. The last time we were standing on this beach, in this very spot, we were going through some really tough times, but I knew in my heart that we'd overcome everything and we'd be standing here all these years later, healthy and with nothing but happiness in our hearts. Elle, these years you've given me have been the ultimate gift of life and I wouldn't trade one single moment of it. We've raised two beautiful and successful children and created a family like no other. Our love is immeasurable and it's forever. We are moving into a new chapter in our lives and I can't wait to write our story and create more beautiful memories together. You are and always will be the love of my life and I want to marry you all over again."

He got down on one knee and pulled a small blue velvet box from his pocket. As he opened it, I placed my hand over my mouth and stared down at the beautiful diamond-encased band.

"Will you do me the honor of marrying me all over again?" He smiled up at me.

He took my breath away. I didn't think it was possible to love him anymore than I already did. But at that moment, a new set of emotions washed over me and it felt like I had fallen in love with him all over again.

"Yes! Of course I'll marry you again." A tear escaped my eye. "I love you so much."

He stood up and brushed his lips against mine as I heard clapping from behind me. I turned around as Collin, Amelia, Julia, Jake, Lucas, Cassidy, Ben, Hailey, Peyton, Henry, Mason, Diana, and Jacob stood there with wide smiles across their face.

"Oh my God! What is going on?" I asked in excitement.

"This is why we couldn't take the private jet," Connor said. "They were all on it and I wanted to surprise you." He wrapped his arms around me as they all came walking over.

"Congratulations, Mom. I was a little worried you'd say no." Collin laughed.

Everyone congratulated us and we headed to dinner at the Beverly Hills Wilshire, where Connor had rented us a private dining room. This man, my husband and the love of my life, never failed to surprise me.

*A Forever Family*

As we finished dinner, Connor stood up and called Collin and Julia to come stand by him. They both gave him a strange look as they walked over to him.

"What's up, Dad?" Collin asked.

The waiter walked over and handed Connor a large brown envelope. Connor looked at his son and daughter and smiled.

"This is for both of you." He handed the envelope to Collin.

"Daddy, what are you doing?" Julia asked with nervousness.

Collin opened the envelope and took out the papers, examining them carefully.

"Dad's retiring and handing Black Enterprises over to us," he said as he looked at Julia.

"Dad, no," Julia said with sadness.

"It's time that I let my children take over the family business. I've groomed you both for this day since the day you were born and now the time has come for you to take over. I'm retiring and your mom and I are going to do some traveling."

My heart ached when I looked into my children's eyes and saw sadness that their father would no longer be at Black Enterprises.

"Dad, I don't know what to say. I mean, I'm thrilled to be taking over, but I'll miss you there."

"Yeah, Dad. We're going to miss you."

"It's not like I'm moving out of the country or the state, for that matter. I'll always be there for both of you."

Collin and Julia both hugged Connor and tears were shed. Not only by us, but by our friends and family as well.

"I want to thank all of you for coming tonight and sharing in the special news and joyous occasion with us. But this is where I must leave," Connor spoke.

I looked at him in shock. "What do you mean you must leave?"

"It's the night before our wedding, baby, and it's bad luck to see the bride on her wedding day."

I was confused. He had me in a whirlwind of confusion. "Huh?"

He placed his hands on my hips and his forehead on mine. "We're getting married tomorrow on the beach. That is why all of our family and friends are here. Everything's already been arranged and tomorrow, we will renew our vows."

"But—"

Mason walked over, handed Brayden to Jake, and placed his hand on my back. "I know what you're thinking, Elle. You're thinking about how you don't have a dress, shoes, jewelry, flowers, makeup, etc. But not to worry, queen bee, I've got everything covered. I picked the most fabulous dress for you to wear and I know you'll love it! So say good night to sexy daddy and let's go back to my place. I can't wait to show you everything."

"I can't believe you did all this. Actually, I can believe it because that's the kind of man you are. I love you so much, Connor Black, and I can't wait to marry you again."

"And I can't wait to marry you." His lips locked with mine. "Now go with Mason and I'll see you tomorrow. This is hard enough."

## Chapter 48
## Ellery

The dress Mason chose for me was perfect. He had really outdone himself with this one. As I slipped into my white, strapless, slim line gown with the notched neckline, I felt like a princess. My hair was done in a loose updo with a few cascading curls and fresh flowers perfectly placed throughout.

"Mom. You look gorgeous!" Julia smiled as she kissed my cheek.

"Doesn't she?" Mason said.

"Thank you. I can't believe how fast all this is happening."

"Daddy's been planning this for the last two months. I'm really surprised you didn't find out. I thought for sure Peyton would have spilled the beans."

"I asked her about it last night and she said she wanted me to be surprised for once in my life. Isn't that what I told her at her birthday party?" I laughed.

There was a knock on the door and Collin walked in. "Wow, Mom. You are stunning." He walked over and kissed my cheek.

## A Forever Family

"Thank you, my sweet boy. Shouldn't you be with your father?"

His lips curved into a small smile. "I'm walking you down the beach."

Tears formed in my eyes and Mason noticed. Running to grab a tissue, he handed it to me.

"No. No, Elle. Don't you dare. You'll ruin your makeup."

I dabbed my eye with the tissue as Collin held out his arm. "No tears, Mom. I'm proud to walk you down the aisle and hand you over to Dad."

I threw my head back because I started to lose control of the tears.

"Collin, stop talking to her. You're making her cry," Mason said.

"Sorry. I don't mean to."

"I'll be okay. Just give me a minute."

"Clarissa, come here! We need a makeup fix stat!" Mason yelled across the room.

After Clarissa fixed my teary eyes, we walked out of the room and took a limo to the beach.

****

## Connor

Julia took her place as Ellery's maid of honor and I waited for Collin to walk my wife down the aisle and take his place as my best man. As I looked beyond the people that had gathered to come watch us renew our vows, I could see my beautiful bride on the arm of my son. I promised myself that I wouldn't get emotional, but seeing her standing there, dressed in white, I couldn't help it. I swallowed hard as the music began to play and they started their journey down the aisle. She was even more beautiful today than she was all those years ago. As they approached, Collin kissed her cheek and gave her hand to me, then took his place by my side.

"You are so beautiful, Ellery."

"So are you, Connor," she whispered with a tear in her eye.

We stood before our guests as the minister said a few words and we happily renewed our wedding vows. I slipped the band on her finger and brought it up to my lips.

"With this ring, I thee wed," I spoke.

She took my hand and slipped on my wedding ring and brought it up to her lips.

"With this ring, I thee wed." She smiled.

"You may kiss your bride, Connor," the minister spoke.

I leaned in and our lips tangled into a passionate kiss. Our guests rose from their seats and clapped as we embraced each other. After taking what seemed like a million pictures, we headed to the Beverly Hills Wilshire for our reception dinner.

It was a night full of celebration and one that would forever be in the memories of our family and friends.

## Chapter 49
## Connor

*Two Years Later...*

What can I say? Ellery and I spent time in Spain, Paris, Italy, and the Caribbean during the past couple of years. Our travels got cut short because Collin and Amelia got pregnant and gave us the surprise of our lives. Twins. A boy named Christopher and a girl named Chloe. Both of them were in shock because Amelia didn't even know that twins ran in her family. Needless to say, they had their hands full and needed us. Collin was doing an excellent job with Black Enterprises and he made me very proud. Julia became pregnant again and we had just found out she was having a little girl. We also attended a very special wedding this past year to celebrate the marriage of my brother, Lucas, and his new bride, Hailey. The restaurant quickly became known world-wide and was very successful. So successful that Lucas decided to open another restaurant in Los Angeles. Hailey started her own clothing line and was flourishing in the world of fashion. Both of them were incredibly happy and it was nice to see my brother find someone special to share his life with.

Unfortunately, Ashlyn lost her battle with cancer and passed away a few months ago. Even after everything she had put me

*A Forever Family*

and Ellery through over the course of the years, she had become a changed woman and it was sad to see her life end so quickly after she spent so many years rebuilding her life and reinventing herself.

As I sat at my desk in the penthouse, I picked up the side-by-side picture of our wedding day and the day we renewed our vows. Our story wasn't always perfect. From day one, we had our ups and downs, but no matter what life threw at us, our love was strong and unlike any other that pulled us through. My life changed the day I saw Ellery standing in my kitchen and that was a day that I'd never forget. Even now, I'd stand in the entrance while she's cooking and think about the first words I'd ever spoken to her. "Did I not go over the rules with you last night?" The words which led to our beautiful life together. A life full of happiness and joy and the creation of a family with so much love and such a tight bond, that nothing could ever break us.

We are the Black family and we will continue to live life to the fullest. Our story may have ended, but we know that we'll be in your hearts forever.

The End

*Sandi Lynn*

# A Special Thank you

I'm sure you're all shedding some tears right now as I am writing this. I want to thank each and every one of you who have followed the Black family from the start. What was supposed to be a standalone novel had turned into five full length novels and two novellas because you demanded more of Connor & Ellery's journey together.

The creation of the Black family wouldn't have been possible without your support and I thank you from the bottom of my heart for wanting more of this incredible and wonderful family. The journey I have gone on writing these books for my wonderful readers was an absolute joy and the Black family will always hold a special place in my heart just as I know they will in yours.

If you haven't already done so, please check out my books. They are filled with heartwarming love stories, some with millionaires, and some with just regular everyday people who find love when they least expect it.

**Millionaires:**

Love, Lust & A Millionaire

His Proposed Deal

Lie Next To Me (A Millionaire's Love, Book 1)

When I Lie with You ( A Millionaire's Love, Book 2)

A Love Called Simon

Then You Happened

**Coming Soon:**

Love, Lust & Liam

**Second Chance Love:**

Remembering You

She Writes Love

Love In Between (Love Series, Book 1)

The Upside of Love (Love Series, Book 2)

*Sandi Lynn*

## About The Author

Sandi Lynn is a New York Times, USA Today and Wall Street Journal bestselling author who spends all of her days writing. She published her first novel, Forever Black, in February 2013 and hasn't stopped writing since. Her addictions are shopping, romance novels, coffee, chocolate, margaritas, and giving readers an escape to another world.

Please come connect with her at:

www.facebook.com/Sandi.Lynn.Author

www.twitter.com/SandilynnWriter

www.authorsandilynn.com

www.pinterest.com/sandilynnWriter

www.instagram.com/sandilynnauthor

https://www.goodreads.com/author/show/6089757.Sandi_Lynn

Printed in Great Britain
by Amazon